#4

W9-CMU-456

# Rose's Dream Fulfilled

## Phyllis A. Collmann

Copyright © 2007
Phyllis A. Collmann

**ALL RIGHTS RESERVED**

This work may not be used in any form,
or reproduced by any means,
in whole or in part,
without written permission
from the author.

ISBN: 978-1-57579-359-7

Library of Congress Control Number: 2007930051


For additional copies of this or other
books written by Phyllis Collmann:
pac51@hickorytech.net
712-552-2375
www.collmannwarehouse.com


*Printed in the United States of America*

PINE HILL PRESS
4000 West 57th Street
Sioux Falls, SD 57106

# ∽ *Dedication* ∾

This book is dedicated to my husband Colin,
for fifty five years of marriage and for his
calm strength and his kindness and love.

To my children
Cynthia, Kimberly, Ronald and Melonie

To all of my grandchildren and
great-grandchildren; I love each one best

# ∽ About the Author ∾

Phyllis A. Collmann is a retired nurse. She lives on a farm with her husband of 55 years. This is the fourth book about Rose Donlin. It is a sequel to her first, second and third pioneer book. The first book is called *Rose's Betrayal and Survival*. The second book is called *Rose's Triumphant Return*. And the third book is called *Rose's Heart's Decision*.

Published books:
   *Rose's Betrayal and Survival*
   *Rose's Triumphant Return*
   *Rose's Heart's Decision*
   *Rose's Dream Fulfilled*
   *Kim's Unplanned Sega*
   *Mother's Innocence Proven*
   *Christmas At Our House*

# A Very Special Thank You

Julie Ann Madden      Kimberly Ann Bonnett

Diane Ten Napel      Nicole Collmann

Allen Leekley for the cover picture of he and his horses and the pictures of his horses inside the book. Allen Leekley is nineteen years old. He has loved horses since a young boy. He is patient and kind and is truly a horseman.

Corey James Collmann, my grandson, for being the photographer throughout the book.

# ∽ *Chapter 1* ∾

Rose suddenly felt this confrontation was going to end badly. At this precise time even the seconds were standing still.

Rufus George had no idea how his appearance would change a dreadful situation. At the same time Rufus George stepped out from around the new hospital, Henry Helgens jerked his horse separating Toby away from Rose.

Rose welcomed the intrusion. Toby had no choice but to take his hands and arms away from around her waist, then step back a couple of steps.

In his usual larger than the average man's steps, Rufus George was standing next to Rose.

Rose spoke first, needing to see how Henry would react to this big black man. Rose's voice was firm and clear as she stared directly at Henry saying, "Henry, this is my friend, Rufus George."

This was more than a meeting between two men. To Rose, it meant the survival of a lifetime relationship that Rose wanted so badly with Henry Helgens.

Rose's eyes stared without blinking. Her body was motionless. And then the most incredible thing happened. Henry's face broke into a radiant smile. He leaned forward and reached for Rufus George's hand. Clasping it without knowing the pain he was going to have to endure.

Rufus George with all his enthusiasm gripped Henry's hand. Henry's smile turned into a look of pain. Rose reached over and laid her hand on the arm of Rufus George. He released Henry's hand and while Henry rubbed his hand, the smile on his face returned.

Rufus George opened his mouth in an enormous grin showing the teeth he had and the space where his teeth were missing.

Both men spoke at the same time, and then laughed. Rufus George was determined to speak again. He said, "Ya fiend, me fiend of missy Ose too."

"Yes, yes, I am a friend of Rose Donlin. I love Rose Donlin." Henry responded in a strong voice. Rose had never heard him say that and it made little chills run down her body.

The voice they all heard next was Toby's.

His voice sounded loud and angry.

"I love Rose Donlin and you are not taking her away from me." No one spoke and everyone turned to look at Toby. Toby's eyes were staring at Henry.

Rose's cheeks were bright red and her body was trembling. She could see everyone turning their head and looking at her. Each person was waiting for someone to speak.

Regardless of Toby's words still ringing in Henry's ears, Henry was a strong, determined man. Nothing and no one was going to stop him or get in his way. His plan was to buy a piece of land and build a cabin, marry Rose Donlin and have a big family like the one he was raised in.

Toby was also a strong, determined man. And he would let no one stop him from pursuing the women he loved, Rose Donlin.

Without any warning Toby leaped up in the air and grabbed Henry's jacket. He pulled him off of his horse. Both young men landed hard on the ground. The horses were jumping and then stepping one way and coming back while the men were hitting each other rolling around under the horses.

It had happened so fast, Rose was caught off guard. Rufus George moved first. He bent down and forcefully grabbed each man's jacket and effortlessly picked each of the men off of the ground straight up into the air. Their feet were six inches off of the ground.

*Rose's Dream Fulfilled*

Rufus George had no problem to continue holding the two men in the air.

"Put them down, please, Rufus George." Rose yelled with a deeper than usual voice sound. Rufus George lowered both of the men until their feet touched the ground. Both men made no attempt to retaliate against the huge black man.

Rose turned toward her magnificent horse. With her hands shaking, she reached for the reins. She pulled her horse close enough until she could lift her foot up and into the stirrups. It took two tries before her foot was secure in the stirrup.

She left the three men watching her ride off.

## ❧ Chapter 2 ❧

Rose needed to be alone. She needed time to straighten out all of the mixed up feelings going on inside of her. Rose was so sure the feelings she had for Henry Helgens were true love. Her dreams of being with him forever were what she had wanted.

Now things had changed and she felt confused. Toby was involved in both of their lives. Hearing Toby say he loved her was making her feel guilty for hurting him. And then there was Maude. Rose knew she would have to deal with her when she found out exactly how Toby felt about her. Maude thought of Toby as her son.

As Rose rode back toward the boarding house, the clouds over head were covering the bright sun that had started the day. The little wet rain drops fell gently while Rose's mind replayed the scene she had just left.

The huge horse's hooves made a rhythmic sound making it easy for her mind to drift back and return to a hurtful place.

The sound of Pal barking brought her back to realize she had reached the stable. Swiftly she dismounted.

Leaving her valuable horse in the hands of a young man Rose hardly knew except for the few times she asked to have her giant horse brought out of the back of the stable where he was kept in hiding from the dark-skinned man.

Rose turned to walk quickly to her room at the boarding house. The young man's voice sounded anxious when she heard him say her name. He tied her horse to a fence and hurried toward her. He stood staring at her determined to say something.

"Rose, the sheriff left a message for you. He wanted me to make darn sure you get it," he said.

The stableman was very close to her and wanted to be sure she got the message.

The sheriff said, "He was sorry but he had to let the man go who has been following you, because he had no hard evidence against him, even though the man was accused of shooting at you and your men." The young man took in a deep breath and continued, "The sheriff also told me to bring your horse to his horse barn behind his office and put him in a stall." The sheriff said, "Your horse would be safe there."

In a whisper all Rose could say as his words tore into her mind and heart was, "Thank you."

## ⤳ Chapter 3 ⤳

As she opened the door, one foot was in and the other followed shutting the door quickly and quietly. Pal was moving around the room smelling everything. He made a second smell of one area of the room and made a low angry growl.

Rose stood with her back up against the closed door watching him closely. Then it occurred to her, Pal was telling her someone had been in her room. She looked around to see if anything was missing. The one possession, the possession she loved the most was not standing on the nightstand where she had left it.

The picture of her family was gone and she was sure who had it now.

Rose was also sure she could not stay in this room. Someone else had a key to her room. She was sure he would return. He would not give up.

Rose had taken the picture with her when her father had ordered her to pack her belongings five years earlier. The five years she lived in the cabin with Joseph Higgens the picture had remained in her duffel bag in her bedroom. At that time it had been too painful to look at. But knowing it was there, brought her comfort.

The thought of the dark-skinned man touching her family picture, made her fear turn to rage.

## ❧ Chapter 4 ❧

Rose unlocked and opened her door only enough for one eye to check the hall and the staircase. She stepped out into the hall with Pal next to her leg. The boards in the floor squeaked so Rose was unaware of another door across the hall opening an inch, enough for someone to see the one person he was looking for.

In a few steps she was at Mary's door. Rose knocked quietly hoping no one in the other rooms would awaken. It took several tries of soft knocking before Rose heard movement in Mary's room.

Mary's voice had worry in it, saying, "Who is it and what do you want?" It couldn't be the one person she feared the most. How did he find her?

"Mary, it's Rose, Rose Donlin, I need to talk to you."

The click indicated to Rose, Mary was opening the door only enough to make sure Rose was standing there. Rose slipped in with Pal crouched down enough to almost get in Mary's room before Rose. Rose grabbed at the door knob, closed the door and locked it before Mary could close the door.

The door down the hall also closed when Mary's door closed. He knew exactly where Rose Donlin was.

Rose whispered, "I need your help, Mary. I need it badly." Mary did not hesitate, saying, "Rose, remember how you and Henry helped me?"

Rose Donlin was not a person to ask for help or to put another human being in danger. Also, Rose loved Mary's daughters, Elizabeth and Sarah. Now, she was without meaning to, involving them, too.

The story Rose told Mary was familiar to the fear Mary had in her heart while living with her husband. He was abusive to her and her daughters. When Rose had finished telling Mary about the dark-skinned man, Mary said, "Oh, Rose, your fear is so real and now, I must tell you how I came to marry my daughter's father. He would not leave me alone. One night I was leaving my neighbor's homestead where I worked as a housekeeper. Jesse Rocker followed me. I was walking and running as fast as I could. He caught me. I fought as hard as I could. I was only 15 years old. When I finally told my parents, I knew I was expecting his baby. My parents insisted I marry him, even knowing he was mean, mostly when he was drinking, and he drank most of the time. But, a young pregnant woman had to have a husband.

## ❦ Chapter 5 ❧

The two young women sat silent for a few minutes. Mary's thoughts were how glad it was she was free of what had been a horrible time in her young life. Free to raise her daughters with love and kindness. They would never have to hear unkind or nasty words from a father that did not love them. Henry and Rose had no idea how glad Mary felt when they had stopped at her home that night a few months earlier. Mary had whispered to Henry to take her and her daughters with him and Rose. Henry's concern at this time was what this man would do if he caught up with them. Rose was all Henry could think of protecting. He could not risk Rose getting hurt.

A few months later Henry Helgens stopped at the Rocker's homestead. Rose had sent for Henry when the dark-skinned man was stalking her. He asked Mary if he could rest for the night. Mary knew immediately Henry had stopped once before. He looked at her young face with bruises showing. He also realized the dark bruises came from the back of her husband's hand.

Henry did not see Jesse. He asked Mary where her husband was. She told Henry he was in town.

The real truth was Jesse Rocker was just behind the cabin. He had come home from town earlier demanding something to eat. Mary tricked him into going down into the food cellar to get potatoes for his supper.

Mary had watched as Jesse staggered out the back door. She waited until she knew he was down inside of the cave. As fast as she could, the cave door was closed above him and the hammer she held in her hand pounded nails all around the cave door. All she could hear were muffled swear words coming up from out of the dark cave.

Mary had had her daughters ready to leave when Henry had ridden up to her home. She knew it would be easier for her daughters if they traveled with a man. Her concern was only to keep her little girls safe. She would not stop for anything.

Mary again begged Henry to take them all along with him. She told him, "We can use the buggy stored in the shed." She also offered to drive while he rested.

They left and no one looked back. Mary left with two secrets.

## ∽ Chapter 6 ∾

Rose spoke first, saying, "Mary, I have to find a way to stop this man before he gets to me again. I have to stop him now and forever, once and for all time. I can't stay at the cabin, he's been there. He has been to Maude's cabin. I can't go back there. Now, he's been in my room, here at the boarding house."

Mary stepped close to Rose and spoke in a whisper, "Rose, I can take care of him. Let me do this for you." The rest of the night plans were made between the young women.

Elizabeth and Sarah woke to find Rose Donlin sleeping on their sofa. The plan had to be explained to the little girls. Mary told her daughters she would like them to spend some time with Rose.

"Why, mommy, why," Sarah was clinging to her mother, adamant about wanting only to be with her mother. Both girls were so afraid they would have to go back. Go back to living helplessly in fear of making their father upset. Then seeing their mother cry made them spend more time alone in their room with a blanket over their heads, hiding from him. Mary knew her explanation would make a difference to her daughters. She had to reinforce the fact that they were never going back and that the fear they both felt would, in time, go away.

The small girls sat listening to their Mother. Sarah was perched on Mary's lap while Elizabeth sat as close as she could with her arm entwined through her mother's. Each girl's eyes were fixed on their mother's face.

Mary explained, "Rose has asked me to go out to the Higgens' Hospital. I need to start my job. I need to be there when they open the doors to anyone who is ill. Rose will let me wear some of her clothes. You will never be alone. Rose will care for you both."

This explanation to two little girls by their mother whom they loved dearly was fine. They both sat with their heads down, while their mother dressed. Rose stood watching in silence.

## ⚬ Chapter 7 ⚬

Mary left the boarding house. She was aware of a door opening behind her as she stepped down the staircase. She was wearing a beautiful long blue satin dress. The coat was light weight, fitting for the warm spring day. The hat had blue lace covering her face. Gloves covered the only remaining skin. Pal was jumping and running along side of her as she headed toward the sheriff's stable. The disguise was spectacular.

Rose dressed Elizabeth and Sarah in the only clothes they had. She also put on the only dress Mary owned. The one Mary had taken off to put on Rose's new clothes. The three dresses had been washed many times and each dress was faded and frayed in places. Rose felt sadness in her heart but she knew she would change all of that. She hugged each girl and combed their long hair. Showing the girls love was easy for Rose.

Rose was trying hard not to dwell on the enormous risk Mary was taking.

Mary listened carefully to the steps behind her. She would stop on purpose to look in a store window and the sound of the steps behind her always stopped. She knew from the sound they were wearing cowboy boots. Mary was determined to take the person following her on a long walk. She went in every store. Standing just inside, looking out to see if she could see this person. Each store she left she walked faster and so did the person behind her. The last store Mary entered she quickly closed the door, leaned against it, and turned to her side so she could see out the window. Her eyes were staring and searching. She stood waiting and watching.

Nearly two minutes passed and then Mary saw the man. The description Rose had given her fit the man Mary was hoping to finally see. His hair was black, his skin was dark. He glanced at the store window and Mary saw his cold steel blue eyes.

After seeing him, for the first time, doubt began to creep into Mary's mind. She closed her eyes, took a deep breath, quitting now was not even an option for her. Mary asked the store clerk if there was a back door she could use. The clerk's face showed a strange surprised look but answered, "Yes, you may go out this way."

The man caring for the sheriff's horses was very willing to hitch up the horse Mary asked for. He had not seen a lady dressed so beautifully come to the stable before.

Rose's horse was a beautiful creature. Mary was used to seeing work horses or horses thin and swaybacked, but this horse was special. The minute she climbed into the buggy the horse was very determined to run. She felt the wheels of the buggy were turning before she was ready. She felt only relief. She had been abused, treated badly, made to live in poverty, and most of all a prisoner of condition. The freedom she felt at this moment was unbelievable to her.

She headed the horse out to the edge of town. The sun was straight up, indicating it was noon, the time for the opening of the new Higgens' Hospital.

## ↶ Chapter 8 ↷

It was a short trip. Rose had the hospital built on her land just outside of Oklahoma City. Mary arrived, urging the horse behind the hospital. She tied the big horse to the hitching post.

The back door of the hospital opened. Toby came out first, followed by Rufus George. Toby was first to reach Mary. The smile on his face showed extreme happiness. He was overjoyed to know Rose was safe, and he admired the way she was dressed, and he loved the beautiful blue veil covering and hiding her radiant face.

He wanted only to touch Rose and kiss her beautiful lips. He yearned to put his arms around her and pull her lovely soft body to his. He wanted to feel the warmth of her body.

Toby walked to meet her with fast swift steps and with all of the love he had been storing up for Rose. He bravely encircled her with his arms, and the next few minutes were wonderful, and to him it was worth waiting for. He had waited so long.

Toby opened his month slightly and laid his lips tightly against hers. It happened so fast, without realizing what was happening, she put her hands on his waist. Mary had never felt this tenderness before. The man kissing her was so gentle, and it made her feel feelings she had never experienced before. Her body responded to his. She let him press her body to his. She let his lips remain on hers and kissed him back willingly.

## ☞ *Chapter 9* ☜

Rufus George began yelling, "Ose, Ose."

Toby thought the sound Rufus George was making was a sound of happiness for what he was seeing. It was not. Nothing could be farther from the truth.

Then through all of Toby's happiness he heard a child's voice screaming, "Mommy, mommy." He had not heard a wagon drawn by two horses, carrying a young woman with two little girls, pull up beside the magnificent horse.

Two little girls came running towards Toby. He stepped back releasing the woman he thought was Rose Donlin.

Rose Donlin was right behind the little girls.

The shock to Toby was so painful. His mind was racing and he was trying to understand what had just happened to him and this person he was kissing. Who had he just kissed?

Under the blue veil, Mary was smiling while her face was flushed from her heart beating so rapidly. Her hands were sweaty and her legs were feeling weak.

Rose stood beside Mary and Toby. The little girls threw their arms around Mary's skirt.

# ✑ Chapter 10 ✑

"Rose," Toby was showing such emotion he had a hard time speaking. Then abruptly, he began by opening his mouth and through gritted teeth said again, only louder this time.

"Rose, what is she doing here?"

"Why is she wearing your clothes?" Toby was livid.

Toby had never raised his voice to her. It took Rose a few minutes to compose herself.

"Toby," Rose said softly, "If I had known you would be here, I would have gotten here sooner. The black-haired man is out on the street and he is after me. I'm afraid."

Toby's eyes did not leave Rose's beautiful face. He stood trying to take in all that had just happened and now, hearing about the danger Rose was in again.

Rose continued by saying, "Toby, this was the only way we could think of to fool the black-haired man. Mary put herself in harm's way, just for me. It was a foolish thing to do. But Mary knows what living in danger is. She just wanted to help me."

Mary had stood listening. Then slowly she began to lift the blue veil off of her face while saying, "Toby, I'm sorry this happened to you. The plan Rose and I made was only to trick the dark haired man. Not to hurt anyone else."

Toby had turned to watch Mary.

He looked at a very pretty young woman's face with a slight smile on it and into dark brown eyes.

No one spoke.

Toby's frown left his face.

All he could manage to say was, "Who are you?" He did not recognize her and he knew he had never seen her before.

Rose said, "Toby, let me tell you all about Mary and her daughters." She was appealing to Toby for his understanding.

---

Mary leaned down and kissed each of her little girls affectionately.

"Toby," Mary said, "Please do not think badly of me as I wanted only to help Rose. The man is out there and he followed me down the street in town, thinking he was following Rose." Mary's voice sounded sad.

By this time Toby had became calm. His body was relaxing and he acknowledged Rose's explanation.

It was the day before the Higgens' Hospital was to open. A stately lady showed up. She was just standing in the hall next to Rose's office. Rose heard footsteps and went to check who had entered the hospital. The lady had a small amount of Indian features, with long black hair that had streaks of gray. Her skin was fair and soft looking, not dark from the sun. Her eyes sparkled, they were the color of a beautiful blue. She looked tall and thin in her floor length skirt. She was wearing Indian moccasins. The beads she wore around her neck were made out of polished stones. The band she was wearing around her head was beaded with many colors.

Rose asked the lady if she would join her in her office.

She answered Rose, saying, "My name is Blue Sky. I would like to birth your babies."

Rose stood looking at her and then she remembered something Joseph had told her. He said, "I have a woman living with one of the renters, she was born of a white mother and an Indian father."

Joseph had only good things to say about her. He also mentioned the lady had delivered all of the other renter's babies.

Rose smiled at her and put her hand out and shook Blue Sky's small strong hand.

Blue Sky agreed and left as quietly as she had arrived.

The sounds of horses and wagons parking in front of the new hospital meant people were coming to use the hospital. One-half of Rose's dream was coming true.

Mary took the hand of each of her daughters and headed into the hospital to start her new job. Toby followed her in to help.

## ↶ Chapter 11 ↷

The day was a first for all who worked at the hospital. The people who came and asked for a job worked tirelessly. Rose was excited about seeing the woman come in to deliver the first baby in the new hospital. She helped Blue Sky prepare the woman for the birth. This woman would not lie in tall grass to have her baby like the Indian baby she had delivered.

Henry Helgens had spent the night in Rose's cabin with Rufus George. The two men wanted to get an early start to measure the ground where the Higgens' Library would be built. The library would only be a short distance from the hospital on Rose's land. Toby was to have met the men at the site, and get the foundation measured off. But Toby had wanted to see Rose first. He left to help start the library. Toby crawled up into the buggy. He would leave the buggy at the library site then take the magnificent horse into the woods at Maude's.

At the end of the day and while it was light out, Rose, still dressed in Mary's clothes, took Mary's girls out the back door and put them on her wagon and headed to the boarding house.

Mary remained behind and moved into the room she and her girls would live in while she worked and supervised the hospital.

She felt lonely without the girls to hug and kiss as she had done every night of their lives. She laid her hands out stretched on her stomach. Mary planned on keeping her second secret as long as she could. Her thoughts drifted back to what she had done. She hoped her husband was able to open the cave door. Little shivers engulfed her body. The picture came into her mind of him down a dark, dank cave, and not being able to get out. Even feeling the way she did about his cruelty towards her, no one deserved a cold, starving death. Or was this an exception? She closed her eyes in peaceful sleep.

## ⁃ Chapter 12 ⁃

The dark-haired man couldn't have found a better hiding place. Only one nurse was there all night. He had followed Mary and had watched from a distance.

The nurse lit the lamps attached to the wall outside of each room giving a small amount of light in the long dark hall. The rooms were completely dark on the inside. If someone needed help, the night nurse would light a lamp in their room.

After dark, the dark-haired man found a way to get into the underground rooms. He pried open a window and slipped in. He stayed all night in the coal bin. He also made sure he could sneak in at night and out just before light. While the nurse was busy taking care of her patients in the morning, he could slip out the window. He slipped a piece of leather, laid it flat under the window so it did not lock. The window closed enough that anyone walking by would not notice the unlocked window.

*Rose's Dream Fulfilled*

During the middle of the night when everyone was sleeping he removed his cowboy boots and crept into the kitchen and ate all he wanted, then, returned to the coal bin.

He knew Rose was in the building. He had followed her from Oklahoma City and he also knew she had ridden in a buggy drawn by his horse. Early that morning he had waited to hear a door open. He opened his door and she had gotten to the staircase. He did not see which room she had walked out of.

The time he spent watching and waiting was to make sure he made no mistake when he finally caught her and took her to Mexico. This time he would make her his woman.

The second day started and Mary did not come out of her room until it was light out. The dark haired man had crawled out of the window easily while it was still dark.

## ☙ Chapter 13 ❧

Rose woke to hear Elizabeth and Sarah whispering under their blanket.

She was unknowingly hearing a very bizarre, unbelievable story. Elizabeth had not told Sarah about Mommy's secret, but Sarah asked Elizabeth some questions about where their father was. She also hoped he never came here. Elizabeth repeated a warning several times to Sarah.

"Sarah, you must never tell or talk about it to anyone. Mommy could get into a lot of trouble and be taken away from us. Mommy does not know I saw her. I saw her follow our father to the cave."

"Didn't our father get the potatoes from the cave?" Sarah asked innocently.

"Sarah, you must never ask Mommy about our father. Do you understand?" Elizabeth said, loud enough for Rose to hear the urgency in her voice. "Do not talk about our father anymore." And then Elizabeth added, "You don't want to go back there, do you?"

Rose moved on her cot, letting the girls know she was awake. She had heard enough to realize someone had to go back to the Rocker's homestead and look for Jesse.

## ☞ Chapter 14 ☜

Each of the girls took her turn washing and dressing. Rose combed and braided their hair. She slipped into Mary's dress and put on a rather large bonnet. She also put on an apron over her dress, making her body size look larger.

Rose took time to lock the room, and then met the girls at the bottom of the staircase. Holding each of the girls' hands she hurried along the street to the stable.

The buckboard was ready and she wasted little time heading it out of town toward the hospital and new library.

Rose had kept her head down not looking right or left. Then as the wagon rolled past the general store she turned her head only slightly. The man she saw made her draw in her breath and quickly look at the reins in her hands. The reins snapped against the back of the horse's back. The girls were hanging on because suddenly the horses were running at high speed.

It only took a small tug on the reins, and the horses were taking them in a different direction toward the Higgens' Library instead of the hospital.

The many renters were there working long hours to build the library for Rose Donlin. The first person walking toward her was Henry. Rose asked the girls to remain on the buckboard.

She hurried to meet him so the girls would not be able to hear their conversation. She wanted only a few minutes alone with him and longed to feel his arms around her. Nothing could stop the next few minutes of passion. He did not even notice how she was dressed, her old faded dress and the big floppy bonnet. All he saw was the woman he loved. The woman he had chosen to spend the rest of his life with. He would settle for no one but Rose.

On his face was the familiar smile that she had come to love while on the month long trip they had shared together.

He approached her and gently took her face in his hands pressing his lips against hers. Her pulse was beating rapidly. She lifted her arms around his neck and squeezed him to her. Her body was warm for the love she wanted from him.

Henry spoke in a whisper saying, "Please Rose, marry me."

"Oh, Henry, I would marry you today, I love you so much. But first I need to tell you about Jesse Rocker."

Rose explained to Henry what she had overheard. She was adamant about the need for them to do something.

It was then she asked if he would make a fast trip back to the Jesse Rocker homestead. "It is so important, Henry," Rose told him and then said, "Please stop at the general store for all of your supplies. Henry, I'll ask Toby to go get my horse. The trip can be made faster on my horse."

Rose had always worked well with Toby but the situation made it difficult now.

She walked into the frame of the library with Henry close behind. Rufus George and Toby looked up. Toby's response was clearly as it had always been. Nothing would stop him. He was close enough to put his arms around her, pinning her own arms to her sides. Toby was hugging her and then kissed her on the cheek.

Henry painfully showed how furious he was. He wanted to fight Toby. He stepped as close as he could before Rufus George stepped in front of him.

Toby released her from his grip.

Rose tried not to show her resentment. She chose to act as if it had not happened and  expressed to Toby how important it was for him to bring her horse so Henry could make this trip. The conversation was going well until Rose mentioned Henry's name. Toby showed only hostility as he walked toward his horse.

## ⌀ Chapter 15 ⌀

Rose could hear the girls behind her laughing and giggling. They had witnessed first, Henry's affection to Rose, then To-by's display of love toward her. They had seen so much since leaving their unhappy home.

Crawling up into the buckboard, Rose smiled at the girls. They were trying to hide their giggles by covering their mouths with their little hands.

Rose tied the horses up to the hitching post behind the hospital. She lifted one girl at a time off of the wagon. The back door opened, and Mary appeared looking lovely in Rose's clothes. Elizabeth and Sarah ran to her as she knelt on her knees to hug and kiss them. Rose stood and watched this wonderful display of the greatest love there is.

Rose knew the trip she was sending Henry on was what she needed to do.

Mary took the girls to her room while Rose checked to see if the cook had all of her supplies from the general store in Oklahoma City. She did not expect to find the lady so upset and angry. Rose walked into the kitchen and heard the cook say. "Well, can you beat that? Someone has been in here during the night. They ate a large part of my dinner for today. If I get my hands on them, they will need to be in the hospital. They left dirty handprints in my clean kitchen."

Rose tried to calm her, the best she could by saying, "I'll take care of it." She left with the cook still complaining and threatening.

Rose walked through the hall, checking the rooms. The nurse on duty was working to make everyone in the rooms comfortable.

She opened the door to the underground rooms and holding her lantern slowly went down the staircase. It was quiet except for the creaking of the boards over her head. The first room was the food supplies because it was closer to the kitchen. She opened the door. Everything was neatly stacked on the shelves. Directly across was the laundry room. Rose had purchased two wringer washing machines. The dryer was the rope tied from one end of the room to the other. Also, rope was tied between posts outside to hang clothes to dry.

The next door she opened was the room that the large stove was in. Pipes from the stove were connected to each room, supplying heat when it was cold weather. Along side of the stove was a door leading into the coal room. The coal could easily be scooped into the stove to heat the entire hospital.

With her lantern she opened the door and stepped in. She held the lantern high out in front of her. The coal pile looked different to her. Not like it should have looked when the men scooped it in through the coal chute. It looked as if chunks of coal had been thrown up to make room along one wall. And as she stood and studied it, she could see it was under the window that a pile of coal remained, and then where she was standing, a path had been made.

Rose took a couple of steps closer to the coal and squatted down with the light. It was as if her eyes were drawn to look between some big chunks of coal. It was then she saw a pile of cigarette butts. Looking closer she could see the remains of the angry cook's food.

Someone was staying and hiding out at night in the coal room.

No one must know. Rose needed time to think of a plan and she also needed Henry to be part of the plan. So before doing anything, she would wait until Henry returned.

Rose looked for the man who came to clean each day. She found him and instructed him about a lock she wanted on the outside of the coal bin door. Also she wanted some chains attached to the wall on one side of the wall inside of the coal room.

She also needed one more lock applied to a door and the lock was needed on the inside of Mary's door. Mary needed protection now more than ever.

Then Rose added "No one must know; no one."

Rose walked directly back into the cook's quarters. She informed the cook to make no change, to leave food as if she did not know of the visitor in her kitchen at night. Looking at the cook, Rose said, "Do not talk about this to anyone."

## ⁓ Chapter 16 ⁓

Rose was right. Henry's trip was fast. He had not stopped to sleep. She was also right about the swiftness of her big horse.

He took the same route back to Jesse Rocker as he had taken to bring Mary and her daughters into Oklahoma City.

As Henry got close to the homestead, he slowed the horse down. It was late afternoon when Henry pulled up in front of Jesse's cabin. He dismounted slowly and tied the reins around a broken post that was leaning toward the ground. The ground was full of trash. Large weeds and thistles grew up around the homestead.

Henry made his way to the door. If Jesse had gotten out of the cave, Henry's fear was getting shot. Being locked in a cold cave could trigger any man like Jesse to be hostile.

He knocked on the warped door. The noise coming from inside was swear words and the sound of Jesse stumbling to the door. Henry felt a sense of relief. At least Jesse made it out of his imprisonment from the food cellar.

Mary could not be accused of killing him now.

The door opened and Henry was not prepared for the horrible condition Jesse appeared to be in. His clothes were dirty, he needed a shave. Jesse held onto the door for fear of falling because his body was shaking and he could not stand still.

Jesse's outburst was loud and he leaned close to Henry's face. He yelled, "You old son of a" then stopped and yelled, "Come in and have a drink." His voice sounded angry.

Jesse let go of the door and grabbed Henry's coat, then pulled so hard they both stumbled into the cabin. Jesse was boisterous saying, "Someone locked me in the cave. They wanted me to die. Do you know who locked me in the cave?"

Henry was right about fearing this man. Jesse's rifle was leaning against the chair he sat in. Jesse could be a very dangerous man. "No, no, I do not know," Henry finally answered his question. Henry hoped Jesse never remembered who had tricked him into the cave.

Before Henry left to return to Oklahoma City, he wanted to loosen and remove the nails from the cave door. If Jesse told his story, or he remembered and told it was Mary, he would have no proof.

The room the two men sat in was in complete disarray. Several big brown empty distilled liquor jugs lay on their side on the floor. Many of Jesse's uneaten meals remained on the table. The odor was rotting food and Jesse's lack of bathing.

Jesse began to cough and it sounded to Henry, Jesse's insides could come flying out any minute. His face turned more than a red color. It was purple, and Henry noticed Jesse's lips were a dark blue color. His breathing was loud and labored.

The cabin showed no signs of anyone else living there.

Henry was not leaving until he knew what Jesse was going to do about Mary and her daughters. Up to now, Jesse had not mentioned their names.

Jesse leaned his head back in his chair swearing. Henry sat listening and heard him say, "I'll get who ever did this to me." And within minutes Henry heard the rhythmic sound of Jesse sleeping.

Henry rose from his chair and as quietly as he could, crept across the floor to the kitchen and out the back door. The cave door was open and lay on the ground with the hinges in- tack but also the sharp end of many nails protruding upward from the top of the door.

Henry found a rock and began pounding the nails back out. He reached under the cave door and pulled each nail backward and put each one into his coat pocket. Mary had not spared the number of nails.

Looking down into the dark cave, Henry felt an urgency to go down into the damp cellar. He felt forced to know the tormented situation Mary was in to send this man into this bone cold damp dungeon. Henry wanted and needed to make some sense of why Mary couldn't have contacted the sheriff.

Henry found the steps slick from the mud tracked up from the floor of the cave. He stood on the floor of the cave trying to see in the darkness. He tried to adjust his eyes quickly.

Jesse had committed his last cruel treatment against Mary and her daughters. She had to be desperate.

Going into the cabin with as little noise as possible, Henry took one step up on the ladder to the loft where the innocent girls slept. The only thing in the loft was two straw mattresses. On the floor were pieces of small girl's clothing. One small garment caught Henry's eye. He recognized it from having so many little sisters. But the difference was small red spots in the center of the garment.

The fence like rough boards kept the girls from falling off of the loft. Also a chain was attached to the top board. Henry checked to see what the chain was for. He pulled the chain straight and then realized it was to lock the girls up in the loft.

An overpowering rage began to consume Henry. He needed to get out of this cabin now before he did something he knew he would regret.

Carefully stepping down the ladder he wanted to get away from Jesse Rocker. Going past the chair Jesse sat on, he looked down at Jesse and saw he was slumped over nearly falling out of his chair. His body showed no signs of life.

Henry tried to lift him up and found Jesse's body limp and cold.

Henry stood for a minute and debated in his mind whether to help Jesse Rocker or walk out of the cabin and start back to Oklahoma City. But then he remembered Rose had sent him here to make sure Mary and her daughters would remain free.

Standing off to the side of Jesse, Henry slipped his hands and arms under Jesse's arms and lifted him up and out of his chair. He dragged him across the room to the bedroom and laid him on his bed. His coughing spells were getting worse and closer together. Henry knew he could not leave Jesse without getting him a doctor or help.

Henry had passed a homestead a few miles back on his way here. He had waved at an elderly woman working in her yard. He headed in that direction to ask for help. It took nearly an hour to reach the cabin. He was welcomed in by an old woman living alone. Henry's explanation about Jesse needing help sent the old woman in a hurry to get all of her medical supplies. She rode easily on the back of the big horse behind Henry.

The old woman mentioned she could hear Jesse coughing as Henry opened the cabin door. She had treated sick men many times before and Jesse was very sick. The old woman was determined to do all she could for him.

Henry was asked to start the fireplace to boil water for preparation to make an oatmeal poultice. The old woman worked for hours over Jesse.

Jesse Rocker did not survive the night.

When the sun rose in the morning, the sky was clear and it looked like a great day for everyone but Jesse. The elderly woman rode Jesse's old horse into town to inform the sheriff. Everything had to be taken care of before Henry left.

The following day five people watched as Jesse Rocker was laid to rest. Henry, the old woman, the sheriff, the undertaker, and a preacher the sheriff had brought along who had never met Jesse. He said kind words over Jesse Rocker which Henry thought he did not deserve.

After Jesse was laid to rest, Henry explained to the sheriff why Mary and Jesse's daughters were in Oklahoma City. Of course, the explanation was not exactly true.

The story Henry told the undertaker took only minutes and then the death certificate was signed as death from pneumonia. Henry asked for a copy but didn't tell why he insisted on having one. His copy would go to Mary. He thought as he folded the paper, Mary would have to choose the time to tell the girls. Henry hoped it would put their fear to rest forever.

## Chapter 17

Henry knew Jesse Rocker was gone. What Rose, Toby, Mary and her daughters did not know, was Jesse Rocker was no longer alive but he still had a hold on them. Even though Jesse was undesirable to Mary, and he would never assault her again. But still he had a firm hold on her.

Henry walked through the cabin one last time thinking he could find something to take back for Mary and the girls. He opened a drawer to discover it was the home of a mother mouse. She had chewed up some important papers. He carefully moved some papers as to not disturb the nest of baby mice. Reading quickly he found the deed to the land Jesse Rocker owned. He continued to search hoping to find a marriage license. The papers were all chewed on, ripped in the creases. Little tears and holes and dark stains from mouse droppings.

Henry finally found a box and began to pile all of the papers into the box out of every drawer he opened. He looked in every cupboard and each drawer. In the very last drawer he opened carefully Henry stood looking bewildered. On the top of a bundle of letters tied with a shoe string, Henry recognized a badge of honor from the Civil War of 1862. He gently picked up the badge and examined it closely.

In quotations it read "Bravery Above And Beyond The Call Of Duty."

Looking down into the drawer, the letters were addressed to Private Jesse Rocker. The return address was a Roberta K. Rocker. Henry felt a certain amount of guilt opening the letter on the top of the stack. He sat down in Jesse's chair and read a letter that made his heartache.

> Dear Son Jesse        1862
>> I am sorry you have to kill boys.
>> Try to eat more. No one hates you for being in the war.
>> Your father is working hard to save the land. If only you can come home soon to help. We use the money you send to run the land and eat.
>>> Mother

Reading the letter made it clearer why Jesse began to drink. He was only a boy fighting in a man's war. Why he had changed and was not the same after the war. Why Mary and his daughters were treated so badly. Jesse refused to forget what he had gone through as a young boy.

Jesse had carried the war home to his homestead.

Reading the letters and being so interested and absorbed into the life of a man Henry only knew for a short period had taken more time than he realized. He had not noticed the weather changing.

First only small streaks of lightning lit up the room, and then when the thunder was loud enough to rattle the worn-out old windows, he stood up. The room was dark until the lightning streaked across the sky. The thunder sounded over head and the rain pounded against the windows.

It was then he began to hear sounds like voices.

---

Trying to remain calm and listen to what he thought were screams coming from the loft. He knew about ghosts and he did not feel like he was alone.

He felt he was being watched and he knew that could not be true.

Something had gone on in this cabin and now he knew why Mary had to get away with her daughters. She had wanted to kill him for it.

The storm suddenly stopped as quickly as it had started. Locking the door as fast as he could, Henry wanted to leave everything behind.

Astride Rose's giant horse, while leading Jesse's only horse, all of the papers along with the medal were in Henry's saddle bags.

## ☞ Chapter 18 ☜

The clouds were all disappearing as Henry rode out into the night toward Oklahoma City. The large bright moon made it easier for Henry to see.

Henry decided he would not reveal everything he had seen and heard. He would make Mary and her daughters start their new lives without having to relive what they had escaped. He wanted to help them get through Jesse's death.

The trip back to Oklahoma City would take more time as Jesse's horse was under nourished. Rose's magnificent horse wanted to run, but Jesse's was unable to move fast. Jesse's horse was being pulled along, and Henry was aware he would have to stop frequently.

When Henry stopped, the horses stood side by side eating grass. One was so beautiful with a shiny coat and stood many hands higher. While the other's coat was rough and its ribs stuck out noticeably.

As the trio traveled slowly through the night, Henry listened and watched for signs of creeks with flowing water. The water was always a welcome sight. The giant horse drank first, vigorously swallowing, then lifted his head high. Jesse's horse submerged his entire mouth and nose into the water, gulping the water. Henry waited patiently for each horse to get their fill.

Pulling back and starting again, it was understandable to Henry they were moving slower. The older horse was breathing harder. Henry suddenly realized he had to stop and let him rest. Jesse's horse was exhausted and Henry could not let him die on the trip.

Henry found a grassy spot to rest in. The older horse was first to lie down. He lowered his head while bending his front legs then as his knees to his front feet touched the ground his back legs bent backward and he fell to the ground on his stomach. Henry watched as the old horse began to slowly lean his body back on his side, flopped his head flat on the grass, as his legs went out stretched in front of him.

Two little girls would need to take good care of him.

## ⁓ Chapter 19 ⁓

Rose started her day with Henry on her mind. She made no changes in her routine and she also explained to Mary that a lock had been attached to the inside of her bedroom door at the hospital.

The cook was getting more irritated but was willing to continue to do as Rose asked. The night nurse was trying to remain calm during the long night hours, knowing a man was lurking and loose in the halls of the hospital. She tried to think about her patients and to prepare the medicine she needed to give, but she found herself stopping and listening to any small noise.

And then she heard footsteps, they sounded as if they were coming closer. She tried to remember what Rose had told her. "Whatever you do, don't panic. He is after only me; he will not hurt you."

She opened a drawer slowly trying not to make any noise. She wrapped her hand tightly over the object Rose had given her.

Out of the darkness came a small boy's voice, saying, "I need to go to the bathroom, would you light a lamp for me?"

Her hand covered her heart while she took in a couple of deep breaths. Then with the other hand she laid down Rose's revolver held tightly in her hand.

## ⁓ Chapter 20 ⁓

Early the same evening, after Mary had kissed her daughters goodnight and helped each one up into the wagon with Rose driving the team, Mary had finished her day's duties and went hurrying into her room. She placed the lock securely as Rose had shown her. Then with no hesitation she removed all of Rose's clothes she was wearing. The night gown was such a welcome relief. Mary did not know how long she would be able to get into and wear Rose's dress. Everyone would soon know her second secret and she needed to tell her little girls before they over heard someone say something to them.

The story she planned to tell the little girls would be the truth but she would not ever tell them everything. Especially the afternoon their father came home after a morning of drinking in a tavern in town. Jesse made the girls go up into the loft and yelled for them to "stay up there." What followed next was punishment for Mary, and she knew if she fought him he would hurt her more.

Before Mary would let him fall asleep, she pleaded with him to go to the cave for potatoes and she would make him supper.

The hammer to pound the nails was laying exactly where she had placed it along with many nails. What Mary did not know was Elizabeth had looked out of the only window in the loft and had seen and watched what her Mother had done. Elizabeth refused to let Sarah look out the window.

Mary's body felt as if it were crying for sleep. It was only a few minutes, and she was in a deep sleep. Mary's room was very dark. Morning was still a few hours away. At first it was only a tap and then it became louder bringing Mary to open her eyes. Then she tried to figure out where the noise was coming from. Someone was outside of her door. She heard a voice and she heard, "Rose, Rose, I know you're in there, open this door now or I'll kick it in."

Mary sat up slowly and then crept across the floor. She leaned against the door with her ear pressed on the wood.

She heard him shift from one foot to the other. He knocked softly but firmly and said again, only this time in a gruff whisper. "Rose, you open this door before I kick it in."

Then Mary heard his foot steps move quickly away from the door. Seconds later a soft voice said, "Mary, are you ok? I thought I heard a voice in this hall."

"Yes, yes, I'm ok, I didn't open the door," she said.

Mary heard the nurse walk away. She knew she would have to tell Rose when she arrived in the morning.

Rose arrived with Mary's daughters and the little girls were happy, talking and laughing, to see their mother. Rose enjoyed seeing the change she had witnessed in the girls. But they were not healed completely because it was almost impossible to separate them. Rose had also noticed when she put them to bed they laid so close to each other while holding hands. Sarah would not let Elizabeth out of her sight, and Elizabeth acted very protective of Sarah. Rose also noticed when the girls talked to each other, they always whispered so softly no one else could possibly hear what they were saying. Rose hoped with Mary's new life, the girls would eventually forget their life up to now.

## $\infty$ Chapter 21 $\infty$

Mary was explicit on her explanation of the happenings during the night hours. Rose thought she needed to put the girls somewhere safer. The dark-haired man was getting closer and acting more daring. Time was so important, and Henry was not back yet from Jesse Rocker's. Rose was determined to wait for him.

The ride out to Maude's was not pleasant. The girls sat on the buckboard beside Rose with their arms around each other and stared straight ahead. They did not whisper to each other like the other rides they took with Rose. Mary had explained to her daughters, she did not know Maude but Rose did, and they would be safe.

Rose hoped the meeting would go well. She also hoped Maude did not come out of her cabin pointing her gun at them because she did not know Rose and the girls were coming. This was not a place that two little girls would find enjoyable but they would be safe.

The horses slowed down as they reached Maude's homestead and then stopped. Rose climbed off of the wagon and tied the horses to Maude's hitching rail. She gently lifted each of the little girls to the ground.

Rose had no idea what would come next.

Hidden from view, Maude had first heard the wagon coming and then stood very still and watched each little girl being lifted off the buckboard. She stepped out from behind the cabin and the girls saw her.

Rose had never experienced what the girls were going to do, nor had she ever seen a reaction like she saw from Maude. Rose felt something moving at the back of her dress. And then she realized the little girls were crouched down. They had crawled under her dress. Little hands were around her legs. Rose was not going anywhere.

The biggest surprise was about to happen. Maude was smiling. Never had Rose witnessed Maude smiling.

Rose was determined to move toward Maude before this situation became ugly and Maude's smile left her face for good. Rose took a small step forward with her left foot.

From under her skirt Rose heard the scuffling of little feet. When she stepped forward with her right foot, the movement under Rose's skirt started again.

Rose heard Maude speak, and the voice was soft and kind, not the voice Rose heard the first time she came here. "Come in and have some homemade bread and jam with a glass of milk." This brought the two little girls out from underneath Rose's dress.

Maude waited until the little girls were close enough, then she opened her arms and pulled each small girl to her and hugged them. Then she took the girls into her cabin, leaving Rose behind.

Rose waited to give Maude time to talk to Elizabeth and Sarah. When she entered Maude's cabin, both girls were sitting at the table and each had a slice of bread with jam on it. A large glass of milk was also in front of each girl.

Maude looked up at Rose and said, "Please, let the girls stay with me for a while. Please, Rose." This was more than Rose had even hoped for. She kissed each little one and then hugged Maude and said. "I'll be back in a few days. This is the best place for the girls right now."

## ⸺ Chapter 22 ⸺

Rose closed the cabin door behind her with a small amount of sadness. The girls had once again been taken from their mother.

The horses appeared not to feel the same urgency to return to the hospital as Rose felt. The team's steps were in perfect match and no amount of coaxing to run was working.

Rose was a short distance from the new library when she could see a rider coming toward her. Her first thought and hope was that it wasn't the dark-skinned man. Rose leaned down to feel under the buckboard seat moving her hand around until she felt something steel and cold.

She squinted her eyes to get a clearer look at the rider. She was sure now it was Henry Helgens. All of her fear left her body and mind, she felt only of being in love with this man. Rose continued staring in the direction of the rider. She saw a tall man sitting on her magnificent horse. He rode with strikingly skilled professionalism.

Then, just as the vision of Henry Helgens appeared to Rose, the vision disappeared and Rose knew it was because she needed him so desperately. The vision was only in her mind.

## ⚬ Chapter 23 ⚭

As Rose approached the library, it stood with bricks covering it completely. Rufus George had taught the men the delicate ability of mixing, grinding, burning and regrinding measured amounts of limestone and clay. He taught them the patience of letting the bricks cure. His father had passed along the craft after learning it from his plantation owner in 1824. The rooms and shelves were still empty but Rose would fill them after she caught the dark-skinned man.

Toby appeared out of nowhere just as Rose stepped into the first empty room. He opened his arms and laid his hand on the back of her head and pulled her to him. Holding back with all of the strength she had, did not work. She could feel his warm breath on her forehead just before his lips covered hers. He made no mistake this time; he knew exactly who he was kissing.

Just as he pressed his lips on Rose's lips, she slid down Toby's body, first to her knees and then onto the floor as Toby moved back and tried to stop her. Rose Donlin had gone to a place of complete blackness.

Toby carried her easily to her buckboard and reached the Higgens' Hospital within minutes.

The nurse on duty was of Spanish descent. She directed Toby to the room which was located next to Mary's room. When Rose was laid on the bed, the nurse kindly asked Toby to wait in the hall. The nurse proceeded to undress Rose and slip a hospital gown on her. She noticed how extremely thin Rose was. It looked to the nurse as if Rose was starving. What the nurse did not know was Rose had not eaten in two days since finding the person she feared so much was hiding in her hospital.

Rose's blonde hair had grown back to the length below her shoulder. Her blonde hair spread out over her pillow. Unlike the nurse whose hair was black with her beautiful creamy dark skin.

The nurse, in her broken English said to Toby, "You must go now because Rose needs to sleep to get well." Toby's concern showed on his face and he firmly asked. " When can I see her?" Without answering, the quiet nurse closed the door.

Toby reluctantly left, only wanting to sit beside Rose's bed.

# ∽ Chapter 24 ∾

The remaining hours of the day slipped by while Rose, who was completely exhausted, slept the entire day. She woke to drink a cup of soup provided by Mary. Then within minutes returned to a deep sleep. Mary had wanted Rose to tell her how Elizabeth and Sarah were doing with Maude, but that would have to wait.

Darkness sent Mary to her room and she slid the lock into its place on her door.

The room Rose was in was dark because the hall lamp was hanging too far away to give the room any light. Rose slept soundly.

Then while it was still dark, she opened her eyes. Without the slightest movement she was aware of someone standing next to her bed. Without being able to see, a hand reached out and touched her hair, and then moved down and touched her face. Her body had been warm under her covers. Now she was rigid, cold and could not move. The hand moved around over her face. Rose lay very still with her eyes closed. Her instinct was to lash out and push the person away, and then jump out of the bed. But another hand was around her arm and she was sure she could not get free.

The hand on her face was rough, calloused and it smelled of dirt and cigarettes. He leaned close enough for Rose to smell stale liquor on his breath. He moved his hand slightly and his fingers were around her neck and then down onto the top of her chest making getting help impossible.

The noise coming down the hall made the intruder step back, turn and leave without making a sound. Rose remained numb. The nurse came into the room carrying a lamp and laid her hand on Rose's arm. Rose could not speak. The nurse asked if she could do something for her. Rose could only move her head side to side. The secret must be kept until Henry returned.

Toby had left the hospital and decided Maude needed to know about Rose. He knocked lightly on the cabin door. This was the first time he had ever gotten to her door without Maude greeting him with her large rifle. When he stepped up to her door, his first thought was she was not in the cabin. He had never heard anything coming from Maude's cabin since he first saw her when he was four years old. Toby opened the cabin door very slowly.

What he saw made him not believe what he was seeing. Maude had an arm around each little girl and they were sitting on her lap in the rocking chair. Maude was telling them a story about Toby. She told them how very much she loved him as if he were her own son. Maude looked up at Toby and smiled.

The wrinkles of age showed on Maude's body along with the life of guilt. But today Toby thought he saw a change. Something of a glow, something he had never seen before. Her face had gone from an ashen grey to a small amount of soft pink. The sadness in her eyes was gone.

Toby sat down at the table while noticing how the two girls had been clinging to Maude since he came into the cabin. He also noticed the girls were holding hands.

Toby's voice sounded soft and calm as he told Elizabeth and Sarah how happy he was to see them spend time with Maude. The girls appeared to relax and they agreed to sit next to Toby while he drank a cup of coffee. He spoke and kidded with them. The girls needed and liked the attention they were getting but Elizabeth never let her guard down. No one, especially a man could get close. She was four years old and grown up to her responsibility of caring for Sarah. Sarah did not move before looking at Elizabeth. A nod was all she needed from Elizabeth.

# Chapter 25

The nurse informed Mary, "Rose is here." Mary immediately took a few steps out into the hall and turned into the room Rose was in. Mary's concern showed on her face and her body was trembling when she reached Rose.

Mary's gentle voice was comforting when she asked Rose to come to her room. She whispered, "Rose, you can use my daughters' bed while you are here.

Rose was safe in the room that had a lock on the door. The room had a small amount of light coming in from the early morning sunrise.

Trying to hurry was becoming harder for Mary. Dressing in clothes too small had become almost painful. Mary slipped out of her night gown. She was not aware the small amount of light was shining on her body. Rose was sure Mary did not realize she could see a change in Mary's figure. The silhouette revealed Mary's breasts were much larger than they looked in Rose's dress. Mary laid her hands on her swollen stomach and now Rose knew Mary's second secret. Her secret was growing.

# Chapter 26

The following day Toby left the library after working all day. He bolted up over the wheel of the buckboard and headed into Oklahoma City and to the general store. Once he was there, he was feeling excited. His mind was on Maude and two little girls. He was not sure why. The first purchase on his list was for Maude. He picked out some material for a new dress. He was sure she had not had one for a very long time.

*Rose's Dream Fulfilled*

Candy was at the top of the list for the girls. Also he had noticed both needed new boots. The need to take care of the little girls felt so strong.

When he arrived at Maude's, both girls were very happy to get candy. The giggles and little squeals made Toby happier than he'd been for awhile.

This reaction that Toby watched from Elizabeth and Sarah was very unusual. They both seemed to relax and just play as they sat near the fireplace with their legs folded under them. The girls sat very close to each other and whispered softly.

The material he had brought back for Maude was beautiful and she said, "The prettiest I have ever had."

## ∽ Chapter 27 ∾

Henry had timed his day of travel and made a guess he could be back in Oklahoma City within one more day. The horses were getting used to one another. Henry felt the younger

horse had slowed down as if he realized the older horse would never make it to Oklahoma.

When they stopped to rest, Henry watched as the younger horse nuzzled up to the tired worn out old horse and would stand close. Without being told, the young horse would back away to let Elizabeth and Sarah's horse lie flat on the ground for a night of rest.

Henry had searched and found the spot for a camp in a secluded and wooded area. He started a small fire and opened a can of beans. His food would last only one more day.

Henry spread his bedroll out on the ground under a large tree. The blanket was big enough to lay on and pull the edges over his legs. His day had started before dawn and now it was dark again with millions of stars glistening over his head. The birds were still awake and noisy. The little animals were still racing here and there. A gentle breeze moved the limbs and leaves making a comforting sound.

He lay down and closed his eyes. His body was ready for sleep, but his mind was thinking of Rose. He imagined her warm soft body lying next to him. He felt her soft hair on his cheek, and he could smell her clean skin.

A deep sleep lasted through the night and into the morning hours. The old horse whinnied and Henry jumped to his feet.

The first few seconds Henry's mind did not grasp the impact. Suddenly he knew exactly what had happened during the night. He had been robbed.

Everything was gone, but the old horse.

Rose's beautiful horse, her saddle. His saddlebag with Jesse Rocker's Medal of Honor for his little girls. The death certificate of Jesse Rocker. The one day of food he had left.

The old horse tried to get up. Henry rocked him back and forth until he was able to get him upon his feet.

Now instead of one long day of riding into Oklahoma City it would take two and one-half days of walking with the old horse. Henry left the wooded area leading the old horse. He walked until he found a homestead. The family agreed to let Henry leave the old horse if he promised to come back for him. The old horse meant nothing to anyone but two little girls. He would never just leave the old horse.

Henry was more determined than he had ever been to first get back what had been taken from him, and then get back to Oklahoma City and Rose Donlin.

He was walking with the sun to his back making it easier to walk fast. He walked as fast as he could for as long as he could then he would slow down. He heard a wagon coming up from behind him. Henry stepped out in the middle of the trail making the horses slow down and then stop.

The homesteader told Henry he was going just to the nearest town. Riding in the wagon gave Henry a chance to rest, and it moved faster than his walking.

After Henry left the wagon, he continued walking through town. The main street had horses lined up along the hitching post. He looked up and down both sides of the street. And then he saw a big horse much taller than the ones he was tied up next to. The line of horses were all tied securely in front of the town's tavern. Henry crossed the street and slowly walked between the horses to make sure.

He opened the saddle bag and he already knew what he would find. The Medal of Honor was there along with Jesse Rocker's death certificate.

Untying the reins and then quietly backing the big magnificent horse out into the street. He mounted him as fast as he could to get out of town.

He did not look back but he heard someone yell. It took only minutes and Henry was out of town. The relief he felt was overwhelming while he clung to the saddle horn. When he was completely out of town Henry turned the giant horse and rode on the outside area. He rode back to the homestead where he had left the old horse that belonged to two little girls. He was not going to stop now until he reached Oklahoma City and Rose Donlin.

## ᗫ Chapter 28 ᗥ

Rose tried to get up; she sat up in bed. Her mind was ready but her body was crying for food and rest. She lowered her weak body back down on the bed and covered up again as she was cold. Rose wiped away the wetness from around her eyes.

Mary had made her rounds and then returned to her room to see Rose.

Rose asked Mary to ask the man that cleans in the hospital to come see her. She had made up her mind. She could not wait for Henry to get back. Rose had to catch the dark- haired man now.

The message Rose sent was delivered as she had ordered. Toby and Rufus George came immediately to the hospital.

Rose talked to Toby first. She explained she thought Mary could be in danger being in the hospital at night while the dark-haired man was stalking Rose. She also added, "Mary needs to talk to her daughters." She continued by saying, "I would like Mary to stay at Maude's with her daughters at night."

"Toby, you need to take Mary out to Maude's cabin after work so she can stay over night and then pick her up in the morning and bring her to the hospital to work during the day." She repeated again. Mary's daughters need her. Rose's voice was raspy and just above a whisper.

Up to now Toby had just stood listening. His eyes never left Rose's face. He was looking into her beautiful blue eyes. His mouth opened slightly wanting to say something.

Rose mentioned one more duty she would like him to do for her. She said very slowly, "I would like you to stop at the general store with Mary so she can purchase some new dress-es.

Toby had been ok up to this point about Rose's wishes, but this was not what he expected. A confused look came over Toby's face, and he yelled. "Why does she need new dresses? Mary can wear yours." Toby sounded agitated.

"Toby, please trust me." Rose whispered. Toby's head dropped down and then he nodded before he walked out of the door.

## ~ *Chapter 29* ~

Toby worked the next day at the library knowing he had to be at the hospital on time so Rose would know he was doing exactly what she had asked him to do.

Rufus George also continued to do his work the entire day and did not talk to anyone about the conversation he had had the day before with Rose. But it was noticeable on his mind. He worked by himself and talked to himself at times. When it was lunch time, he sat across the room from the other men to eat, including Toby.

Looking at his pocket watch so many times in the afternoon was unusual for Toby. But today was different, and every day from now on. After he finished his work, he splashed water over his face and hurried out to the buggy.

Toby pulled the horse up to railing in front of the hospital and jumped from the buggy when he saw Mary come through the front door. He had no idea why he had the urge to help her into the buggy.

Neither spoke on the ride to town to the general store. Toby jumped out first to make sure he could get around the buggy to help Mary.

Once inside Mary went toward the dresses hanging on hangers. Toby watched as she walked past the dresses with low necklines and tight waists. She stopped and took down two dresses with a high collar, straight to the floor, full of material with no waistline at all. She took two with different colors but made the same. Then she picked out two floor length aprons to completely cover the dresses. The bonnets she chose were large and would not only cover her head but also her face. Toby shopped for food supplies to take to Maude's because she had three more people to prepare food for. He helped carry all the purchases to the buggy, and after placing each item behind Mary's seat, he helped her up into the buggy.

No one seemed to be watching the two of them start out of town, but by the time the buggy had reached the edge of town, Toby was sure they were being followed. Mary turned her entire body to see only enough to recognize who was riding so close he could have stopped them and taken Mary, thinking it was Rose. But the person behind, knew it wasn't Rose in the buggy. The minute Mary turned only slightly he knew. He pulled his horse out around Toby's buggy and headed toward the hospital.

Toby cracked the whip over the horse and turned him into Maude's lane.

## ⌒ Chapter 30 ⌒

Toby opened the door and held it open. Mary stepped in and walked to the rocking chair. The girls squealed and ran to their mother. Elizabeth and Sarah's excitement was overwhelming. They both jumped up on their mother's lap. The giggles and high pitched squealing of laughter was loud as Mary sat trying to calm them down. She waited patiently because she knew two days for two little girls is a long time to wait before seeing their mother.

Mary began talking to Elizabeth and Sarah in a whisper.

Toby and Maude walked to the cabin door intending to go outside and leave Mary alone with her daughters.

Elizabeth's outburst of yelling, "No, no, no, Mommy. No. Daddy will be so mad." Then Sarah screamed when she saw how upset Elizabeth was.

While sobbing and talking in little short breaths, Elizabeth said, "I don't want to take care of another baby, Mommy."

Maude and Toby stood in silent shock. Neither one could move. Mary's second secret was out now.

Mary's face was pale and looked strained as she listened with a guilty disbelief for what she had done to her daughters. Mary had, without thinking this would ever happen, put all of Sarah's responsibility on Elizabeth so she could keep Jesse from getting upset and getting angry when Sarah cried. Elizabeth had spent her time keeping Sarah away from their father.

The little girls sat with their faces embedded in their mother's dress and only muffled sob sounds could be heard. Mary kissed each one on top of their head over and over.

Mary began to explain so each little girl would understand. She did not mention their father. She reassured Elizabeth she would not have to take care of their new baby. Mary said, "I will care for this baby. I just want you and Sarah to love this baby."

Rocking the girls seemed to help comfort them and they became quiet. It was then Elizabeth said, "Mommy is Daddy out?" Mary did not answer.

## ∽ Chapter 31 ∾

Rufus George was the last man to leave the library. He checked and locked all of the windows and then walked toward the front door. The air felt cool after the sun went down. The building had no light inside or outside. The darkness engulfed the halls. The empty building sounds were eerie.

The noises Rufus George heard were faint footsteps in the dark hall behind him. Rufus George stopped and listened carefully. He stood very still. The boards in the floor were all new and any pressure applied the boards would squeak. One small squeak and Rufus George knew precisely where the intruder was.

Rufus George did not move because he was a very large man; the floor would tell the intruder exactly where he was. Minutes went by and Rufus George heard the intruder take a few more fast steps away from where Rufus George was.

The back door slammed shut; the intruder had left the library.

Rose listened to Rufus George as he told her who he thought it was in the dark hall of the library. Rose solemnly agreed. She had already decided who it was.

## Chapter 32

Early in the morning Toby pulled up in front of Maude's cabin. Mary stepped out of the cabin wearing one of her new dresses. Toby thought she looked so thin in the dress even knowing what he did. He noticed how tired she looked. Her face had no color. Mary's eyes were red and puffy. Toby imagined she had cried herself to sleep. Her steps were slow and she walked with her head down.

Toby reached her as she began to climb up into his buggy. He lifted her up easily and returned to pick up the reins and drive her to the hospital.

Mary surprisingly said, "I appreciate your doing this for me." Toby felt very emotional and no words seemed fitting. He couldn't believe he felt this way. Why?

He watched as Mary walked up the path and opened the door and stepped into the hospital. He had so badly wanted to ask her what Elizabeth had meant when she'd asked her mother, "Is daddy out yet?" He wondered if Jesse Rocker was in prison.

## ᔆ Chapter 33 ᔆ

Henry Helgen traveled the last twenty miles on foot into Oklahoma City. Even trying to get Rose's big horse to walk slowly was much too fast for Elizabeth and Sarah's old horse to keep up. Henry walked, leading the two horses slow and meticulously.

He knew it would take longer but this was the only way the old horse would make it to Joseph Higgens' homestead. He let the horses graze on grass along the path. Any time Henry saw a stream, he would lead the two horses off the path and let them drink and rest.

When Henry saw light from the town of Oklahoma City he stayed away from Main Street. He led the two horses around the town and onto Rose Donlin's land to Joseph Higgens' run down homestead.

Henry put the two horses into the corral. He fed and watered them and locked the gate behind him. He took the saddlebag with all of Jesse Rocker's valuable papers with him. Telling Mary and her daughters would be hard, but the papers to prove Jesse Rocker was gone, would make it easier.

He stepped into the empty cabin. He entered the bedroom that Rose Donlin used the five years she had lived in the cabin with Joseph Higgens. The instant he laid his head on Rose's pillow he felt her presence there. His exhausted body put him to sleep for hours. The night was gone and Henry continued to sleep through the day and into the next night.

He woke suddenly with someone breathing close to his face. Rufus George, with his huge body, was leaning over Henry.

Henry did not look the same, not like the last time Rufus George had seen him, before Henry had left for Jesse Rocker's homestead. His hair was long now as was his beard. His face was nearly all hidden. The clothes he had on were worn and needed to be washed.

"Rufus George, you just scared the heck out of me." Henry said, coming up off of the bed with his hands made into fists.

"Henny, Henny, it's you, so gad you hir. Wat mells, ya eed a baff? Rufus George said while sticking his hand out to shake Henry's. Henry reluctantly put his hand out and at the same time squinting his eyes expecting the pain to begin. Rufus George had a smile on his face and he covered Henry's hand and gently shook it. Henry's face turned into a big smile.

The two men sat close enough to touch. They sat with their eyes directly on each other. Rufus George left nothing out, telling Henry everything that had happened since Henry had been gone.

Rufus George began speaking and Henry immediately asked him to speak slower. Then he made him repeat several words as Henry could not understand them. He did not want to miss one word.

Rufus George told him about the hospital's intruder, about the library's intruder, about Mary and her daughters living at Maude's cabin, about Rose getting sick, and the wicked visitor coming into her room. Rufus George left the information about the hospital's coal room until last.

Henry was quiet for a few minutes and then he said, "Rufus George, I would like to keep my return here a secret. I don't want the dark-haired man to know I'm looking for him." Henry went on to tell Rufus George to hide the two horses. No one must know I'm back."

Henry told Rufus George to go about his days work at the library. He said, "I will only go out at night to search for the man who is making Rose's life miserable and making her live in fear. I must catch him and punish him."

Henry wanted to see Rose Donlin and tell her how much he loved her but that would have to wait.

## ↷ Chapter 34 ↶

The old horse would be his way of traveling into Oklahoma City. No one would recognize the old horse. He waited until the sun had gone down. His first stop was the bar that had the most horses tied up to the railing. He walked into the loud and noisy room with a player piano blaring. Smoke filled the air. No one looked up or even noticed him. He picked a spot at the very end of the bar. A couple men moved farther down the bar.

The bartender took his time to ask Henry if he could help him, giving Henry time to search the faces of all the men in the bar. Henry looked at each face and no one looked like the man he was looking for. He drank a small glass of beer leaving a little beer in the glass because his plan was to visit every bar.

The next bar he entered was nearly the same. The room seemed to Henry to be darker than the first bar. He also noticed a few women entertaining customers. A couple of the women looked at him but Henry had not bathed for weeks. He did not comb his hair before coming into town. So no one took a second look at him. He was someone even the men moved away from because of his odor.

Henry stood alone in a corner and he slowly checked over every man in the bar. The man he was searching for was not there. No one watched as he shuffled bent over and passed through the swinging doors to the street. He entered the street and walked in the direction of the next bar.

Henry looked across the street and he could see a man standing in the shadows of an alley. It was so dark in the alley, yet Henry thought the man had been watching him. The man was smoking a cigarette, and when he put it in his mouth and inhaled, the ambers lit up a small amount of the dark-looking man's face.

Henry stood a few minutes and then started across the street toward the man. He was half-way into the street. He never took his eyes off of the man but without being able to stop him, the man disappeared down the dark alley.

Henry got to the unfamiliar dark alley. He hesitated before going in. He was just inside of the darkness when he heard two men whispering ahead of him. He stopped, paused and then thought better of going any farther. He had too much to live for than to take a foolish chance of getting badly hurt or killed. He would not jeopardize his chance to spend the rest of his life with Rose Donlin. He turned and as his back was to the alley, he felt an instant pain on the back of his head. Henry was falling, and his body was limp as he hit the ground hard.

The sun was almost up and the alley was getting light enough so people on the street could see Henry lying on the ground in the alley. But no one wanted to help a dirty, disheveled unknown man. His old worn hat was lying a few feet away. Blood was seeping out of a large open area on his head. His dirty hair now was mixed with blood.

Henry tried to wake up but the pain kept pulling him back into darkness and relief. His head was hurting with pain like he'd never felt before. He tried to wake up. He was feeling hands on his body, he was being rolled over roughly and he could hear voices but it wasn't English, so he could not understand anything being said. The voices sounded desperate, whispering in harsh tones.

Suddenly he heard his name the only way Rufus George could say it. "Henny, Henny, is dat ouu"? Henry could only moan and answer, "Take me to Joseph's cabin."

With no effort Rufus George picked Henry up and carried him to the buckboard. He wasted no time getting out of town and onto Rose Donlin's land.

Rufus George had found Elizabeth and Sarah's old horse where Henry had left him. He tied the old horse behind the wagon. The wagon moved slowly out of town pulled by the mules Rose had purchased for Rufus George.

Rufus George wanted to get out of town. He did not want to draw attention to himself. This was the first time he had been into Oklahoma City because he did not feel welcome with the stares. He had heard people yell awful things at his family while he grew up. The beating Rufus George had taken outside of town made him realize his color was a judgment of who he was. Not his love of people. Not his kindness. Not his good heart. Only the color of his skin.

By the time Rufus George reached Joseph Higgens' cabin Henry was awake. Inside of the cabin Rufus George insisted Henry take a big drink out of a liquor bottle left in the cabin from when Joseph lived there.

Henry was yelling, "No, no," but Rufus George was so much stronger than Henry. He held him firmly and poured the liquor time and time again into Henry's mouth before he started to take care of the protruding gaping site.

This was not the first time Rufus George had cared for a wound. He first learned from his mother how to take care of knife wounds. He remembered well when he was a boy being awakened during the night when a man on the plantation was beaten badly or knifed because of saying something wrong or doing something that made the owner or a family member angry. They would always bring the injured man to his mama and daddy's shanty.

The plantation owner would wait until everyone was asleep to punish the unsuspecting slave. He would break into the man's home and punish him in front of his family. If the man had open areas that needed to be cleaned and pulled together, or bad bruises that needed cold cloths applied, they would take him to Rufus George's mama's shanty for help. All the slaves soon discovered where they could go for help.

The stricken man would be brought in and laid on the kitchen table. The lantern would be lit but turned down as low as it could so it could not be seen by the plantation owner. Everyone talked in a low whisper.

Rufus George was told just how to hold the lantern while his mama worked over the slave. He turned the wick down as far as it would go without going out. The lantern had to be held next to the injured person so his mama could see and treat him.

The windows in all of the shanties were covered with blankets as soon as the sun went down. This was the only way the slaves had any privacy in their shacks.

Rufus George laid Henry on Joseph's bed next to the fireplace and then hurried to build a fire. Henry had lost a huge amount of blood. Rufus George hoped the liquor was helping to numb the gruesome pain. It was moonshine his daddy used to help the slaves while his mama worked as fast as she could so she did not get caught because the consequence would be worse for everyone in the shanty.

Rufus George held his hunting knife into the burning ashes. He cut Henry's hair off only around the wound. Cleaning the open area was extremely painful for Henry.

Henry's teeth were clamped together tightly. Rufus George could hear them grinding while he worked on him. The liquor helped but the evidence of the pain was clear to Rufus George. Rufus George continued to prepare the wound to begin its healing. When he was finished Henry slept the rest of the day.

Rufus George left for work the following day leaving Henry sleeping soundly. When he left work, he checked all of the rooms and checked all of the windows at the library. The building was empty.

When he left work, he went straight home to the cabin. As Rufus George walked into the cabin Henry was sitting at the table. Both of his eyes were black and his hands were under his chin holding up his head. Blood was showing on the wrap Rufus George had used as a bandage for Henry's head.

Henry's voice sounded angry, "I was robbed. They took my papa's pocket watch and my lucky stone my little brothers gave me. Whoever hit me also robbed me."

"Do you think this was a robbery by someone other than the dark-skinned man?" Henry asked slowly with a look of pain on his face.

Rufus George did not answer.

He sat down next to Henry and started to unwrap the dressing on Henry's head. Henry's head slowly went down until he laid it on the table.

# ❧ Chapter 35 ❧

Toby had been living at his family's homestead helping his mother since his father had died. Each morning he left at the same time to pick up Mary to take her to the Higgens' Hospital. He would return at the same time and take Mary to Maude's cabin after he left his job at the library.

He didn't understand why his feelings had changed. He had been irritated about the extra duty Rose had insisted he do. He had not wanted to do this for someone he did not know.

Now he was eager. Now he was always early. He would pull the buggy up in front of Maude's cabin and then wait for Mary to come out. After work, he would pull up behind the hospital and just sit and wait.

Mary was enjoying the quiet rides with Toby. They would exchange a few words. She never wanted to talk about Jesse Rocker to anyone so that was the only thing she would not talk about. Mary loved to talk about her daughters and Toby was a good listener.

The buggy pulled up behind the hospital a little earlier than usual. Mary noticed nothing different as she crawled up into the buggy. Toby had always helped her into the buggy. Always, except today.

The buggy was moving before Mary looked over at Toby. When she did, the face she saw was not Toby.

Mary yelled, "Stop, stop. I'm sorry. I need to get out. You need to stop; let me off."

The dark-skinned man did not look at Mary, and he did not answer Mary. He did not stop. He whipped the horse into a fast gallop.

Mary could not jump out for fear of hurting the baby she was carrying.

---

*Rose's Dream Fulfilled*

The dark-skinned man knew exactly who he had in his buggy. He had big plans for Mary and the baby she was carrying. His plan for Mary was to make lots of money.

He really wanted Rose Donlin but she would have to wait until he returned from Mexico. His plan was to take Mary to his family until the baby was born.

The dark-skinned man and Mary were many miles down the road when Toby pulled up behind the hospital. He sat waiting to see Mary come out of the door. He always helped Mary up into the buggy as he planned to do today.

Each time the wheels went around they were taking Mary farther away from her beautiful little girls. She held on with one hand. Her worry and concern was the baby she was carrying, so she held her unborn baby with the other.

The night was so quiet with millions of bright stars so far above but not enough light for Mary to see where they were going. She guessed she and her baby were being taken to Mexico. She had had this helpless feeling many times before living with Jesse Rocker.

Mary was aware of the dark-skinned man pulling back on the reins and then the horse was moving off of the path into a wooded and overgrown weeded area. She could see the roof of a small wooden building. The closer they got, she could see a dingy small hut.

## ❧ Chapter 36 ❧

Toby walked up the path and into the hospital thinking Mary was working late finishing up some extra work.

The first nurse he met, he greeted her and then asked for Mary. The nurse was smiling until Toby said, "I have been waiting outside for nearly an hour."

With no hesitation the nurse headed into Mary's room where Rose was recuperating. Toby heard muffled voices and then instantly he heard Rose raising her voice and now the calm atmosphere of the hospital was no longer calm and serene as Rose had first ordered when the hospital opened. Now she was out of bed in the hall heading toward Toby and she was ordering every room to be searched including the underground rooms, including the coal room. Everyone was franticly searching after the nurse told Rose she had said good night to Mary, and as Mary opened the back door, the nurse had seen a horse and buggy waiting for Mary.

With no hesitation Toby left the hospital and stopped long enough to unhitch his horse from the buggy. He rode bare back until he could get his saddle from home. His second stop was to see Rufus George. He had a revolver but he also needed Rufus George's rifle. Jumping from his horse and flipping the rein over the hitching post he leaped upon the porch. Toby flung open the door and was greeted with a colt .45 and a rifle pointing at him.

Toby threw up his hands and with huge eyes of fear yelled, "Don't shoot, it's me."

The cabin was dead silent while Toby and Henry glared at each other. Rufus George slowly lowered his rifle. He scolded Toby about entering the cabin saying, "Us couda shot ya." Toby's reply was, "yah, yah."

Then Toby walked up close to Henry's face and his eyes studied him including the white bandage around his head.

He took in a deep breath and said, "Henry, is that you? What happened to you? When did you get back? Have you seen Rose? Does she know you're back? Mary is missing. I think the man that has been stalking Rose has taken her and is heading to Mexico. I'm leaving now to find her." His voice sounded shaky and then he said, "I have to find her."

"Wait, wait, you are not going alone and you can't start at night. He knows the way in the dark, we do not. We'll start at day break. I'll tell you everything when I get back from seeing Rose." Then he turned to Rufus George and said, "Get the big horse ready in the morning."

Before Henry left the cabin and rode to the hospital on Toby's horse, he asked Rufus George to cut his long hair off and shave him and then he headed for the creek with a bar of lye soap in one hand and the only clean clothes he owned in the other hand. This was not how he had planned the meeting but he couldn't leave again without seeing her.

Rose went back into Mary's room after the search was completed and wondered how she could tell Elizabeth and Sarah their mother was missing. She felt she was to blame and her heart was so heavy. Her thoughts were tearing her mind apart.

Rose was standing at the window looking out into the darkness. The sky was so full of stars it looked as if there was no room for one more.

It wasn't a loud noise she heard but it brought her mind back to reality. The door was not locked because the man she feared was gone and he had Mary.

The noise made her turn and then she saw him. Without a word tears ran down her cheeks and she could see his eyes were full of moisture. Her body began to tremble, her body suddenly felt warm. She drew in a deep breath and it caught in her throat. She had thought about and longed for this minute for what seemed all of her life.

Henry removed his old cowboy hat and his curly hair did not fall down on his forehead as she remembered each time he had removed his hat, instead he was wearing a bandage.

Her heart began beating faster and she moved to him stopping close to him. Rose reached up and gently laid her hand on his cheek. They stood in their own world of love. Henry laid his hand over hers and slowly moved her hand over his mouth. His lips were moist and warm. She wrapped her other arm around his neck. Henry's head bent down slightly and tenderly laid his lips on hers. Her response was all he had hoped for. **Henry knew he was not leaving that night.**

## ⌒ *Chapter 37* ⌒

Henry left the contents of his saddle bag with Rose. He explained how he hoped in time Elizabeth and Sarah would think of their father as a hero. Also they were entitled to the homestead. He asked Rose to tell Elizabeth her father did not die in the food cellar, if he did not return.

When Henry arrived back at the cabin early the next morning, Toby was ready and impatiently waiting. Rufus George had the big horse ready for Henry with supplies and a large amount of ammunition. This trip was not going to be easy for either man. He worried about Henry and Toby traveling together because this trip was about saving each other's life, finding Mary, and bringing her home safely. Rufus George was not sure if they could do this.

He stood on the porch and told them both, "You no fiht hat ech otter. Ya ear."

Toby yelled, "Let's go; we don't have time for this."

They started by back tracking to the hospital and starting at the exact place where Mary had climbed up into the wrong buggy. Following the buggy tracks was easy at first as it was dry and dusty. The horses moved fast all day and the two men had nothing to say to each other. The communication between them was nodding or pointing. They pushed the horses hard.

The direction they traveled was south out of Oklahoma. Henry was the first to speak saying, "We'll stay out of any big settlements. The dark-skinned man is traveling with a white woman who is pregnant. He does not want to draw attention to himself. "So," Henry lowered his voice and said, "It's going to be a long trip for Mary and her unborn baby. We can move faster. The buggy will have to stay on the trail."

They moved hard and fast. No stops were made until late in the afternoon. The grass was plentiful so the horses were given time to eat and rest. They rode a few more miles and Toby suddenly pointed to the wheel tracks. They both pulled their horse off of the trail and went a short distance and could see the top of the shed. It was then they both got down, tied their horses to a tree, and walked the rest of the way.

Cautiously they crept up to the shed with their hands prepared to draw their revolvers. Henry squatted to feel the burned out fire. He felt underneath the sticks on the ground, it had a tiny amount of warmth. Henry looked up at Toby and said, "Five hours."

Toby walked into the shed. It was so small only one person could sleep in it. Both men exchanged glances. Toby said in an angry sound, "She laid here, he laid on the outside of the closed door. Let's go."

# Chapter 38

Mary never argued with the man. He spoke in Spanish with hand gestures. If he had to repeat his words, he would raise his voice and hands. Jesse Rocker had raised his hands at her many times so she learned not to say a word but to do exactly what she was told.

She waited in the dirty shed until he had made a small fire to make coffee and heat a can of beans for them. She knew she had to eat for the nourishment of the baby.

The night went by one hour at a time because the baby Mary was carrying did not sleep either. It was as if the baby felt its mother's desperate situation. Mary rubbed her stomach gently and hummed hoping the baby could feel its mother trying to comfort it. When the baby stopped kicking, Mary was able to sleep.

The door opened waking Mary abruptly. The man shouted, "Go, go," She crawled up into the buggy. He handed her a hard piece of bread to eat.

The buggy was back on the trail and moving fast. The man was using a whip on the horse.

Mary could have hollered at a couple of men on horseback going in the other direction but she knew it would only mean trouble for her when they stopped that night. Her face was dry and red. Her hair was wind blown. She needed water. Her throat was extremely dry. She was terribly hungry not having eaten since morning.

Her stomach was feeling tight and it worried her. She did not want to go into labor, not here, not now. She did not want to have this baby now; it would be too small to survive. She would lose the baby because of this cruel hateful man, a man who enjoyed hurting other people. This made her more determined than ever to save this baby.

64 *Rose's Dream Fulfilled*

The big horse was always out in front of the horse Toby was riding. Toby was pushing his horse to its limit to keep up. The sun shown all day and the heat was slowing the horses down. Their bodies were dripping with sweat.

Henry pulled his horse off of the path. He could see a stream a short distant ahead and the horses needed to drink. Toby pulled up a few minutes later and removed the saddle off of his horse. Both men rubbed their horses down to cool and dry them off. Neither man spoke.

The dark-skinned man refused to stop. His horse had been running all day in the heat. Mary could tell the horse was slowing down and she could see wetness on its stomach and under the harness. The man used the whip frequently. Mary could see welts on the horse's back. Nothing she could say would stop him.

Suddenly the horse began to trip and stumble. Before the man could stop, the horse dropped first on his front knees, then fell over on the side of the buggy Mary was riding on. It began to pull the buggy over slowly.

Mary quickly braced herself. With the openness of the buggy, she turned and reached out and down to break her fall with her hands and knees.

The man was screaming in Spanish. He threatened her, shouting, "Stay, stay."

Mary lay on the ground and at first she waited to feel pain and then she waited to see what the man was going to do. She lay quiet and felt no pain. The man fell harder than Mary. He jumped up and she watched him grimace with pain from his leg. Mary watched as the man hopped over and kicked his dead horse. Then he slipped and fell.

He got up again and yelled, "Help, help." The dark-skinned man was expecting Mary to help him walk. Mary sat up slowly.

Her mind was dealing with what had just happened and now she must make the right decision.

If she made the decision to run. It wouldn't be fast enough to keep ahead of him. Also she was not alone, she had to make sure her baby was safe. The area was familiar to him. She had no idea where they were.

If she made the decision to help him, he would not change his plan for her. His cruelty went to the depths of his soul and beyond. She had dealt with another cruel man.

Her decision was to stay with the dark-skinned man and when the time was right, she would not hesitate.

His voice was getting louder shouting in Spanish, "Get stick, stick."

Mary tried to stand upon her feet. The first move was to turn onto her hands and knees and then up to standing. Her body was getting heavier each day. She moved to a tree area. The limb she picked would have to be just perfect, perfect to break, bend, or cause pieces to break off and cause pain for him.

Mary knew the time was right.

She stood far enough away, but close enough to hand him the end of the stick. He tried several times to get up and when he did the pain showed on his face. His leg protruded out to the side.

He put his weight on the stick. Mary was sure the steps he took and the pain he endured were in desperation to get her to Mexico. She walked behind him, waiting. The stick would bend slightly with each step he took. Mary looked at the pant leg of his sore leg, it looked tight. The leg was swollen.

She was sure it was broken.

The day was long and walking in the sun felt extra hot. Mary was sure the dark-skinned man was suffering more with each step he took. Late in the afternoon he dropped to his knees and turned and looked at Mary. He could not take another step. His eyes were full of terror.

Mary stood looking down at him. The fear she felt when she first realized she was in the wrong buggy was gone. Her first thought was to make sure he never stood up on his feet again.

Her mind pictured what she had done to save her little girls. Then she had a vision of reaching under her dress, pulling and tugging until her petticoat slipped down to her feet. The white under garment she tore into strips three inches wide. Each strip was used. First she tied his hands together. Then she tied his ankles together. The next strip she tied it around his neck and pulled the end tight and looped it through the strip around his ankles. This was pulling him into a bending position.

Mary was so preoccupied with her vision. Then she heard him.

"Go, go," he shouted franticly at her. The harshness in his voice was outrage. He pointed to a sign on a fence post. It read Sweetwater, Texas.

Mary wanted to stay with him to make sure he didn't get up and walk away. But he continued to yell. His yelling from misery was loud and shrill.

She turned and looked in the direction he wanted her to go. She could not see any settlement. Before leaving him, Mary leaned as far as she could without getting too close and picked up the very end of his stick and threw it as far as she could. She couldn't understand the words he was saying but she was sure he was swearing at her.

The evening was beginning and it soon would be dark. The sun was starting to go down. Mary was tired from riding for many days and yet the dark-skinned man was adamant she walk into the town and bring him help.

It was dark when she walked up the three steps and into the Sweetwater, Texas sheriff's office. Her steps were slow and deliberate so she wouldn't fall. She grabbed a post to steady herself. Her face was dry and sunburned with smudges of dirt. Her long dark hair was snarled and tangled.

Mary lightly knocked on the door and it opened immediately. The sheriff was a large, burly, middle-aged man with a kind face. He reached out and took hold of Mary's arm. He gently guided her to the nearest chair. He held her weight until she timidly sat down.

Mary started to talk and the sheriff interrupted her saying, "Just take your time. Where did you come from? Is your baby ok? What's your name?"

She tried to tell the sheriff everything she could remember. The sheriff's face changed and showed anger. The last thing she told him was where he could find the dark-skinned man. She took extra time to tell him. Mary went into great detail about the area. She told him about the trees and the ditch he was lying next to. She mentioned how dark the area was. "It would be better if you waited until morning to look for him." She said.

Quickly she added, "I have not eaten since morning."

The sheriff was very concerned about her condition. He showed interest in caring for her. He stated he would make her a meal. He jumped to his feet saying, "I'll get you something to drink right away."

The sheriff told her he had a cot in the back room and she was welcome to sleep there. He continued by telling her he would fill the tub in the room for a bath.

"My deputy will be here the rest of the night. There is a lock on the door so you can feel safe." He told her.

Mary thanked the sheriff several times.

# ❧ Chapter 39 ❧

The sheriff waited until he had eaten his breakfast the next morning. He then took Mary some breakfast to the room she stayed in.

The sheriff and one of his assistants rode out of town in the direction Mary had described to him. They rode up to the area and looked at a spot where someone had lain on the flattened grass.

No one was there. They did not find anyone. The sheriff noticed signs that two horses had been there.

The sheriff's assistant questioned the possibility of Mary making a mistake where she had left him, also if she had made this all up and there never was a man who had kidnapped her.

The sheriff rode his horse back and fourth around the area looking carefully at what could have happened to the man Mary told him about.

The sheriff started back into town to tell Mary, but also question her. His assistant was driving a wagon that they had hoped to bring the man into town and take him to the doctor.

The sheriff arrived into town in about half the time he thought it would take and went directly to his office. He said nothing to his deputy. He walked to the back room where he had left Mary. He knocked on the door. He put his ear to the door and could not hear any movement. His hand went out and turned the handle while opening the door.

The smile on the sheriff's face disappeared. The room was empty.

The deputy quickly explained, "Mary's brother came to get her."

# ∽ Chapter 40 ∾

Toby rode into Sweetwater, Texas alone. The street was busy with men, women and children. He walked, while leading his horse, looking and searching for Mary. He asked several people if they had seen a young pretty woman who was with child. No one he asked had seen her. One lady told him to go into the dining room at the boarding house and ask.

Toby went directly to the cook and she was more than willing to talk. She explained to Toby she had not seen her but he might want to check with the sheriff. Toby was curious and asked, "Why?"

The cook said, "The sheriff ate his breakfast and then also ordered a breakfast to take back to his office. He never has done that himself. His deputy always does it if they have someone in the jail."

Toby thanked her before leaving for the sheriff's office.

He entered the office and the deputy asked if he could help him. Toby inquired about his sister who was with child and he was very concerned and worried about her.

The deputy acted glad to see him and glad Mary had a family. He immediately took Toby to the back room.

Toby curtly turned his back to the deputy when he got to the door and thanked him. The deputy nodded his head and went back to the front office.

Toby knocked lightly and opened the door. Mary was sitting on the cot with her hands over her stomach. She was deep in thought wondering what the sheriff would do with the man when they found him and how she would get back to her daughters.

She looked up and slowly rose from the cot. Nothing could have surprised her more. She walked to him as he reached out for her. He kissed her lightly on the forehead. The hug was so comforting to her. Toby could feel the baby pressed up against his stomach.

"Mary, listen to me and you must do exactly what I tell you", Toby said in a whisper. His eyes were large and staring into hers. Mary realized how serious he was.

"Mary, we have to walk out of here now and walk as fast as you can." Toby said, as he took her hand and headed to the front door.

As they walked past the deputy, Toby said, "We're going to get something to eat." The deputy's reply was, "I think that's great."

Toby was pulling Mary as fast as she could go. Outside he grabbed his horse's reins and Toby was leading them to the railroad station. He tied his horse to the cattle car. Then took Mary into the station office and purchased two tickets to Oklahoma City. Also he asked to have his horse loaded on the train and paid extra for him.

The ticket agent said, "We leave in thirty minutes."

Mary sat quietly. Toby was nervously pacing.

Toby grabbed Mary's arm after he heard the conductor yell, "All aboard." The train was filling up fast. Mary slipped in first and sat by the window. Toby continued to be nervous moving his legs and tapping his fingers on the seat. Mary knew something was bothering him badly.

The train began to move and started picking up speed. It was then Mary noticed how much calmer Toby was. She moved from leaning against the window to leaning her shoulder and arm against his. Mary felt safe for the first time since this all started.

She started the conversation by saying, "I miss my daughters so much. I do hope they are not giving Maude a hard time."

"No," Toby said, "they will be just fine with Maude. She is a wonderful caring woman."

They sat quietly for a while listening to the rhythmic sounds of the train. Toby moved his hand and touched her arm. Then he touched her hand. He wrapped his hand over hers. She laid her head back on the seat and closed her eyes. Mary had never met anyone like Toby.

The train was right on time. It pulled into Oklahoma City as night approached. Mary opened her eyes and realized her head was lying on his shoulder. They stepped down off the train looking like a young married couple. Toby held her hand and walked along the train and found his horse tied to a post near the cattle car. They continued on to the stable and rented a buggy to take her out of town to Maude's cabin and her little girls.

## ☙ Chapter 41 ❧

Henry was riding as fast as he could. His sleeping blanket was wrapped tightly around the dark-skinned man and he was lying tied to the saddle over the back of the big horse. Henry was taking him to the doctor at Rose Donlin's hospital. Henry was sure the dark-skinned man's leg was broken and he also thought it could be infected.

Henry and Toby had made the decision to take the dark-skinned man after they found him lying along the ditch. Henry said, "We can keep track of him if I take him back."

"Toby, you can go look for Mary." Henry said, knowing that's what Toby wanted to do.

Henry found this trip much more difficult than he could imagine. He made several stops along the way. He stopped when the creek had plenty of water. First he would dismount and then untie the man. He would lift him off of the horse and lay him on the ground. Next he would unroll the blanket. The man screamed from pain. Henry tried to be gentle while lifting him into the water with all of his clothes on. The pain would appear to ease up. Henry would leave him sit in the cool water. That took much more time than Henry wanted but the man wasn't crying and swearing in Spanish when he was in the water.

Henry prepared the blanket first by spreading it out next to the water. The man tried to get away each time and it ended up the same way each time. Henry was stronger and more determined than ever. He held the man down. He rolled him up while he squirmed and twisted in the blanket and kicked with his good leg. Henry would lift him onto the back of the big horse and tie him securely. The next time Henry stopped it happened all over again and the situation was getting more violent. Henry decided he would not stop again until he was in Oklahoma City.

He traveled all night while the man was verbally loud and abusive. They arrived in the city and Henry pulled up in front of the sheriff's office at noon. The sheriff listened and agreed the man needed his leg cared for.

"He also needs to be locked up in jail to recuperate until the judge is notified of what this man had done. We have finally got him." The sheriff said with confidence, then added, "My deputy and I will ride to the hospital with you. In case you need help."

The sheriff told his deputy to get extra handcuffs and short pieces of rope and repeated, "This man is dangerous. I've tried to keep him in jail but I have never had enough evidence until now."

The minute Henry arrived at the hospital the man began to holler. A nurse heard and hurried to the door and opened it for Henry. The noise could be heard all through the hospital. The doctor came hurrying out of a room with his nurse running behind him.

The doctor was shocked to see a man being carried in rolled, up in a horse blanket. He motioned for Henry to carry the man into the surgery room.

Mary and Rose almost collided in the hall. They both stopped in the door of the operating room unable to go in.

Around the operating table and holding the man was Henry, the sheriff, and his deputy. The doctor was trying to give the man a shot with two nurses assisting. It took several tries before the needle went completely in.

The doctor said, "Let's wait a few minutes until the medicine works." It only took a short amount of time.

The doctor insisted everyone helping wash their hands thoroughly before touching anything in the room.

Henry began to carefully unwrap the sleeping man from the saddle blanket. He let the end of the blanket drop down on each side of the table.

The doctor's face was sober when he looked from one nurse to the other. His voice was stern when he said, "Cut this man's clothes off of him now." Each nurse took a scissors from the tray and started cutting on the man's pant leg. The deputy picked up a scissors from the tray and proceeded to cut the man's shirt off. One nurse laid a folded cloth over the middle part of the man's body so he was not exposed.

No one talked until they all looked down at the man's leg. At first it was only the sound of each one in the room inhaling their breath. Then each one looked at the other in shock. Henry leaned down and picked up the man's pants and checked the pockets and he found what he was looking for. His pocket watch, his lucky stone. It was clear who had beaten him up in an alley in Oklahoma City. He reached in again and pulled out a picture.

"Henry, a small voice coming from the doorway," Rose said, "It's my family picture."

"Clean this "man's" leg before we reset the bone." The doctor said loud and angrily, he continued, "I need more light in here."

Rose left the doorway and returned carrying a lamp in each hand.

The doctor looked at Henry and said, "I am going to need help to get the bone straight. How the hell did this leg get so bad?"

He looked at the sheriff and his deputy and said, "If this man moves, tell me immediately. Also, I might need you both to help."

The doctor decided the man needed a little more medicine. The leg would need a huge amount of pressure applied to it.

The doctor had each man stand by the area where the bone was broken.

"We will start at the bottom and watch me push the bone." The doctor explained. Each man put their large hands on the protruding bone and pushed. The sound was of the scraping and grinding of the bones coming together. Each man tried hard not to cringe. After several tries by each man, they all stood back and looked at the leg.

The doctor's comment was, "It looks as good as we'll get it. Now we'll mix up the cast. The mixture will take about an hour." Then the doctor looked at the sheriff and his deputy and said," If you have to go, we can do the rest."

The sheriff's voice sounded harsh when he said, "Hell no, when we go, he goes with us to jail."

"You can't move this man," the doctor yelled back.

"Yes, he will leave when we leave," the sheriff said with finality in his voice. "You can come to the jail in Oklahoma City to check on him."

Putting the cast on was tedious and complicated. Keeping the leg straight and packing the plaster around it took two hours. When it was completed, Henry left the room and hospital to get Rufus George's team and wagon to transport the man to jail.

As Henry walked past Mary he leaned over and whispered in her ear, "Mary, I need to talk to you. It will be late when I get to Maude's cabin. Please have the girls in bed when I get there." Mary looked puzzled but agreed.

Rufus George was at the library when Henry arrived. His team and wagon were tied up to the hitching post. Henry left the big horse for Rufus George to ride back to Joseph's cabin.

Several big blankets were laid on the bottom of the wagon box for the man to lie on. He was still in a deep sleep when Henry, the sheriff and the deputy arrived at the jail. The cell the sheriff put the man in was the one located most distant from the sheriff's desk because he expected the man to be very noisy when he awoke.

## ∽ Chapter 42 ∾

The ride to Maude's cabin was a quiet time for Henry. Time to think about what he would tell Mary. He realized he was the only one who knew the truth. He also knew what he told her would have a lasting effect on Mary and her daughter's lives. He hoped Mary and her daughters would not have to live the rest of their lives remembering only bad things about Jesse Rocker.

Henry was late getting to Maude's cabin but Mary was up waiting for him. The girls were in bed as was Maude.

Mary opened the door, and Henry stepped in carrying his saddle bag. She asked him to sit at the table next to the fireplace. The room was dark except for the light from the burning logs.

Henry asked Mary how she was feeling. Her answer was, "I'm so glad the dark- skinned man is where he should be."

The first paper Henry took out of his bag was Jesse Rocker's death certificate. Henry told Mary, "Jessie Rocker is gone."

Mary began to tremble and said in a shaky voice, "Did he die in the ---

"No, no," Henry said, knowing what Mary was about to ask. "He died in the cabin."

"I went for help but it was too late." Henry said, "The woman I asked to help him did everything she could to save him. Jesse died of pneumonia. He is buried next to his parents."

"Did he mention me or his daughters?" Mary's voice was soft almost a whisper.

"Yes, yes," Henry said, "He said he loved his family."

Mary asked again, "Did he say, did he really say he loved his family?"

Henry hated lies. He had been taught not to ever lie but this was one he thought Mary and her girls needed to hear to start a new life.

"Yes, Mary, that's what he said," Henry answered.

Mary blinked as hard as she could but the tears did not stop. They dripped down her cheeks and onto her dress.

---

_Phyllis A. Collmann_                                                    77

Henry was sure the lie he told Mary was what she needed to hear.

Next, he took out the Medal of Honor. Mary had never seen it before as Jesse had kept it locked away. Then Henry gave her the letters Jesse's mother had written and sent to him while Jesse was a boy serving in a man's war. Henry hoped after Mary read them, she would understand why Jesse was the way he was.

The last piece of paper was the deed to the homestead Jesse owned. Mary and her daughters owned it now.

Henry and Mary sat in silence. Each had their own thoughts on how each of their lives had changed.

Henry got up from his chair slowly and walked quietly to the door. He left Mary by herself in front of the fireplace with all of her grief, sadness and guilt.

Henry and Mary weren't the only ones awake. Rose could not get to sleep. Her worry was gone and yet she did not go to sleep until morning. The dark-skinned man was locked up in jail. She had nothing to fear now, she thought.

Her wish was Henry would return to the hospital and to her. Instead he went to Joseph's cabin. The library was due to open in two days, and Henry wanted Rose to get some rest.

## ✑ Chapter 43 ✑

Before Rose left for the new library, she asked the cleaning man to repair the window in the lower room of the hospital that the dark-skinned man had been using to sneak in at night. She also asked if he would remove the chain attached to the wall in the coal room. She wanted nothing in the hospital to remind her of someone who brought danger into the Higgens' Hospital.

The shelves in the new Higgens' Library were being filled with all types of books. Rose had given the library all of her own books. Also she had sent for boxes of books from the catalog. Her love of books and learning was clear. The library would be a wonderful place for everyone, from a small child to the elderly, to come and read or to take a book home.

Rose was extremely happy on the day the Higgens' Library opened the door to all her friends, and all of the people she did not know. People from Oklahoma City came throughout the day making Rose realize how important books were.

The day was mostly clear. The sun was bright and warm with only a few fluffy clouds. The birds were chirping loudly, wanting to be heard. Rose wished Joseph could be here to see the hospital and now the beautiful Higgens' Library. He had loved books, too. She had read to him each night before he fell asleep. She was sure he would be elated over seeing the two buildings with his name printed on the front.

## ❧ Chapter 44 ❧

At breakfast, Mary asked her daughters to go for a walk with her. They walked toward the creek where the clear warm water flowed in its banks on a pleasant sunny day. Elizabeth and Sarah were happy, hopping and running around their mother.

Mary sat down on a blanket she had carried under her arm and laid it down under a big old oak tree. The girls sat down next to their mother. Mary's voice was soft and sounded sad.

She began by saying, "Girls, I have something to tell you about your father. Henry, who is a friend of Rose, was on a trip and stopped to see your father. He told me your father was very ill when he got to our cabin. Henry got help for your father but your father died of pneumonia while he was there."

Elizabeth and Sarah had been sitting with their heads down until they heard their mother say, "Your father has died."

Sarah reached over and took hold of Elizabeth's hand.

Elizabeth's eyes were large and red. She was staring at her mother with a frightened look on her face. She opened her mouth to speak and Mary interrupted her, saying, "Henry said, your father died in the cabin in his chair."

"In Father's chair?" Elizabeth asked in a whisper.

Then both little girls crawled up next to their mother. She put her arms around them to show them they were safe and Mary said, "I love you both very much and I will take good care of you, I promise. Together we will all take good care of our new baby. Together we will all love it and keep it safe."

Mary leaned back and lay down on the blanket with each little girl lying with their head on her arms.

Suddenly, Elizabeth raised her head and yelled, "Toby, Toby come play with us."

Elizabeth was laughing and giggling, and Sarah jumped up from the blanket and ran to Toby. He lifted her into the air and then hugged her. It was at this time the girls recognized the old horse Toby was leading was their old horse. They had

loved the old horse. The horse was the one thing they cried about having to leave. Mary had put them upon the horse's back many times and led the horse around the yard until Jesse became irate about them riding his horse. It was then he refused to let them near the old horse.

Toby told the little girls, "The horse is yours now." Nothing could have made them happier. They both jumped up and down clapping their hands.

Elizabeth and Sarah had always thought the horse was who they could spend time with and talk to and never get scolded. They would sneak out of their cabin and go to pet and talk to what they thought was their own horse. When Elizabeth and Sarah looked at the  old horse, they saw a giant steed. Many hands high, with a straight back instead of a swayed back. Legs that were long and lean. They did not see the weak legs with big knobs on both front knees. They saw their horse with a dark shiny coat, not the rough, crusty, scarred coat he had.

At last they had part of their young life back.

Toby sat down on the grass beside Mary. Everything felt good and peaceful. He was always calm. "Henry told me everything. I want or I would like to help you." Toby whispered to her. Mary looked up to the heaven and was completely speechless. The only noise she could hear was Elizabeth and Sarah playing and talking to their horse. Even the birds, sitting on a limb of the oak tree over their head, sounded happy and carefree.

Mary felt Toby's hand on her arm and then he moved his hand down and took hold of her hand. Hearing that her husband had died, Mary found Toby to be a comfort for her, and to her. A little smile appeared on her face.

## ⌒ Chapter 45 ⌒

The baby Mary was carrying was due in one month. She was aware how alone she was. Nothing in her life was more important to her now than the baby she was going to give birth to and her two daughters. Mary had no one left to take care of her except the friends she had made since coming to Oklahoma City. She knew she would have to depend on Rose for her job. Maude had asked her to stay with her until the baby was born. After the baby was born, Mary knew she would need a place of her own to care for her family. Mary enjoyed her job and working with Rose.

The following morning Rose woke up feeling better and with the dark-skinned man now behind bars. She felt confident her life was just beginning. She was in love and was feeling happy. She wanted and needed to see Henry.

Rose left the hospital and headed to Joseph's cabin. Her heart was full of joy. Everything she saw along the way made her more content than ever before. She noticed things she had never seen or paid attention to before. The grass along the trail

*Rose's Dream Fulfilled*

seemed greener. The fields had been planted, and the crops were growing. How beautiful the country looked.

The renters who rented and lived on her land were all home now after building the hospital and library. Rose took care of each family and their needs.

Rose reached Joseph's cabin as Henry was saddling the magnificent horse. He yelled out when he saw her coming, saying, "Pal and I were just coming to see you."

Her happiness showed in her smile. "I came to take you and Pal for a canoe ride," she said shyly. She was carrying a lunch pail and a blanket.

His response was, "I would like that very much, Rose."

The canoe had not been used since Rose had used it to take Joseph on a canoe trip when he was feeling better. Pal jumped in first as Henry helped her into the canoe and then pushed the canoe into the water. Rose sat quietly watching him. She loved to watch him. He took an oar in each hand and the canoe moved easily out into the center of the creek. The water was calm and Rose put her hand out into the water. She closed her eyes and the memory of the warm water while she swam to her hidden inlet was the only relief she had felt when she first came to live with Joseph Higgens five years ago.

The canoe moved through the water smoothly with Henry's movement of the oars. Rose looked up, and Henry was smiling at her like he had done the month they traveled together.

"Rose Donlin, I love you and I am asking you to marry me for the second time." Henry said it with a kind voice, yet it was with authority.

Rose answered, "Oh yes, Henry, yes."

When the canoe was again tied in its spot, she asked if he would go for a walk with her. Rose had been there many times on the walks she took while living here. It was a place where she could see for miles all of Joseph's land.

"This," she said, "would be a wonderful place to build a cabin for you and me."

Henry took her gently in his arms and kissed her passionately and said, "Could we build it with many rooms?"

## ⌒ Chapter 46 ⌒

Mary had worked all day and tried to ignore the uncomfortable feeling she was having. She had been so busy she couldn't remember if the baby had moved that day. The day started early with patients needing cuts stitched up. Two babies were born in the morning.

In the afternoon a young girl came in alone, and Mary guessed she was approximately fifteen years old. She acted scared and was very timid. Mary was suddenly and emotionally drawn to the young girl whose body was close to giving birth to a newborn.

Mary prepared the girl for giving birth.

She asked, "Do you have someone from your family coming? Is your husband coming soon? Your baby is going to be born soon."

The young girl did not answer only moved her head from side to side then closed her eyes.

Blue Sky came into the room and gave the girl comforting words and then gave Mary her instructions for the girl to give birth. The hours slipped by while Mary worked with the young girl.

Later Rose came into the room to send Mary home and she had told Toby to bring the girls back so they could stay at the hospital with her. Rose was aware Mary's baby was due and she needed rest.

Toby, Elizabeth and Sarah arrived at the hospital after the sun had gone down.

Rose met Toby and asked if he would get help from the sheriff. She told Toby about the young woman in the hospital that had no name.

Rose said, "We do not know where she came from or what her name is."

Rose took the girls into the kitchen, and the cook was happy to give each of the girls a cookie with a glass of milk. Rose put the girls to bed in Mary's room.

Rose went in to check on the young girl. Her labor continued slowly while Blue Sky took care of her. The frightened girl's face was red, and Blue Sky whispered to Rose, "She has a fever and we need to pack her in cool cloths."

Rose could see how serious the condition was of the young girl. She slipped into a white clean apron to cover her clothes. She was ready to stay with Blue Sky until the baby was born.

The young girl who had not spoken a word since she walked into the Higgens' Hospital was very ill, and now she was getting very tired. Blue Sky was asking her over and over to push so the baby could be born. Because the girl's fever was so high, Rose changed the cool cloth frequently.

## ⌐ Chapter 47 ⌐

Maude tried to get Mary to eat a little. Mary explained to Maude she was not feeling well.

"I think my baby will be born before morning." Mary said softly.

Maude had only seen and helped animals give birth, so she thought she had to get Mary to the hospital while the midwife was still there.

That was not the only reason Maude wanted to leave soon. The clouds had started covering the sky late in the afternoon and now in the dark, little streaks of lightening were off in the distance. Maude could hear thunder getting louder and closer over head.

Maude left the cabin and hitched up the horses to her wagon. The horses acted as if they knew a terrible storm was coming. They pranced around making hitching them up take a longer time.

Mary was at the door when Maude came to get her. Maude's bumper shoot was old and worn out with holes in it. Maude grabbed a blanket to wrap Mary in for the ride through a rain storm to the hospital.

The rain started while they crawled up into the wagon. Maude wrapped the blanket around Mary as the rain poured down on them. The sky lit up with the loud claps of thunder. The horses would not wait, they started to run, and Maude was trying to hold them back.

The wagon was jolting one way and then another. Mary was holding on. Every piece of their clothing was soaked and the ride was very rough for someone ready to give birth.

Maude was a small woman but her strength was like a man. She held the horses from running away. Maude pulled the horses as close as she could to the door of the hospital. She jumped down and tied the horses securely, then helped Mary down and into the hospital. Mary's body was shivering from the cold rain.

The nurse met them at the door knowing Mary had come to have her baby. Mary was taken to a room and prepared. The cook came from the kitchen and offered dry clothes for Maude.

Rose was told Mary was ready to have her baby.

The hospital was dark with only light from the small lamps except when the light from the lightening flashed. Shadows on the walls made everyone uneasy. The thunder woke the babies and they began to cry. The rain pounded against the windows.

Rose came into Mary's room with Blue Sky. Mary was sure her baby would be born soon. Blue Sky agreed and asked Mary to rest for awhile.

Mary asked about the young girl and her baby.

Rose told Mary, "The girl is very sick; and we are doing all we can for her."

Just then the nurse stuck her head in the room and called for Blue Sky to "come now."

The young girl lived long enough for her baby boy to be born. The baby was perfect in every way and only Rose and Blue Sky knew.

Rose told Blue Sky she would take care of everything and she did not want anyone in the hospital told. In the morning she would send for Toby to get the sheriff and the undertaker.

The storm continued while Mary's baby's birth was getting closer. A small lamp was the only light in her room. Rose and Blue Sky were ready to deliver Mary's baby.

Mary's delivery of her baby was difficult and she struggled until almost daylight. The baby boy did not take a breath, his body was weak and his lips were blue. Blue Sky worked tediously on him. She ordered the nurse to quickly bring in two pans of water, one warm, the other cold. She would dip him in one and then the other and then finally she wrapped him in a blanket and told the nurse to take him to another room.

Mary called out wanting to see her baby.

"Rose, what is it? Rose, is it a girl?"

Rose was determined to make this as easy on Mary as she could.

"Mary, the baby needs some special care first. You'll have to wait until Blue Sky examines him." Rose told her with a soft sounding voice.

Mary said, "Him?"

Blue Sky was sure about the baby when she took the first look at him. The baby was taken to the same room where the young girl was.

The other baby boy was lying sleeping peacefully.

No one would ever know. Rose would make the exchange and no one would ever know. At least not for a while.

Mary and Jesse Rocker's baby had died. The first few months had been hard on the development of Mary's baby. Blue Sky had told Rose the baby's heart had not developed right and was not strong enough to live. But for along time, Mary would not know this.

Rose walked into Mary's room carrying the beautiful baby boy. Mary was ecstatic with love for her new baby boy. The baby was happy and content to nurse from its new mother's milk.

The girls were told they could go into their mother's room and meet their new baby brother. Rose lifted Elizabeth and Sarah up on each side of their mother. The girls welcomed their brother with kisses and touching his hands. Winding his tiny fingers around theirs. Toby stepped in the room with a huge smile on his face.

Rose stood in the doorway and watched this blessing.

Mary was a devoted and kind mother. She had been through so much in her young life. Rose would take care of this family.

The story was told to the sheriff by Toby about the very young girl and her baby dying in birth. The sheriff explained to the undertaker about the dress provided by Rose that the girl would wear. The baby boy would be wrapped in a new blue blanket. The baby would lie on his mother's chest with her arms around him.

Rose was the only one who witnessed the bodies. She stood alone and sobbed by the sadness she felt.

Rose informed the undertaker where to take the coffin. The burial site would be in Joseph Higgens' family cemetery.

Henry, Rufus George and Toby had the grave open and were there waiting for Rose and the undertaker. The coffin was lowered down by the men and Rose read out of Joseph's family bible. She read Psalms 51: 1-6.

1 Have mercy upon me, O God, according to thy loving kindness: According unto the multitude of thy tender mercies blot out my transgressions.

2 Wash me thoroughly from mine iniquity, and cleanse me from my sin.

3 For I acknowledge my transgressions: and my sin is ever before me.

4 Against Thee, Thee only, have I sinned, and done this evil in thy sight: that Thou mightest be justified when Thou speakest, and be clean when Thou judgest.

5 Behold, I was shapen in iniquity; and in sin did my mother conceive me.

6 Behold, thou desirest truth in the inward parts: and in the hidden part thou shalt make me to know wisdom. Amen.

The cross read "April, 1885, Mother and Son."

Rose stood looking down at what she had done. She remembered going to Mary about the dark-skinned man and Mary had not thought about the danger she was in but had thought only about protecting Rose.

Some day Rose would tell Mary what she had done.

## ⌘ Chapter 48 ⌘

The vast acres of land Rose owned made her heart swell up in her chest at times. The bank in Oklahoma City was growing rapidly. John Fitzpatrick had made a visit to the Higgens' Library.

Joseph had owned one-half of the bank in Oklahoma City and now it also belonged to Rose.

John had walked into the library unannounced and surprised Rose. He had entered quietly. Rose had her back turned busily putting books away. She turned and he was smiling at her.

She couldn't help but think back when she was only seventeen years old. Rose had arrived here lonely, hungry and with only one dress, the dress she was wearing. She had not wanted to come here. Her father had sent her without asking if she would like to go.

John Fitzpatrick had been the first man she had seen that made her realize she was a grown woman. She felt feelings she had never felt before. He was so handsome. He was dressed so well in a suit. She was used to seeing men in dirty overalls.

Immediately upon seeing him only once, Rose wanted John to be the man her father had sent her here to live with and marry.

Joseph had asked John Fitzpatrick to pick her up from the train and bring Rose Donlin out to his cabin.

"You look wonderful, Rose." John said, while moving closer to her. He reached for her hands and lifted them to his lips. He pressed his lips upon the back of each of her hands. She tried not to feel anything. She smiled warmly and said in a soft voice, "John, you are so kind to come here."

"Rose, I need to talk to you about the banks growth. The bank has grown so fast, we need more room. We need to build on soon." He said.

Rose paused, then quietly answered.

"If you have a plan to expand the bank, please do what you have to do, John. I would like to be informed of all of the progress, if you don't mind."

Rose turned and picked up a book. She hoped he would leave without wanting more from her.

"Thank you, Rose I'll make sure you know exactly what I'm doing in the bank."

She heard the door open and then shut. Her head slowly went down and she laid it on top of her desk She closed her eyes. All of the last few weeks came flooding back into her mind. Her body gave into her emotional state. She slipped into a fitful sleep, full of turmoil. She woke with a jerk and the vision of her dream made her think maybe what she had done was the best solution to give Mary's new baby a better life with a mature mother and two little girls to love him.

The library halls were getting dark as Rose locked the door. It was only a short distance for a brisk walk to the Higgens' Hospital.

# ∞ Chapter 49 ∞

The sheriff looked up from reading the papers on his desk. The elderly couple standing before him looked sad, and was dressed poorly. Their clothes looked soiled and faded. They showed their age by their dry wrinkled sunburned skin. The man's hair hung down under his hat to his shoulder. The woman's gray hair lay limp and snarled to her waist. They both were thin and both looked emaciated.

The man opened his mouth to speak. "My wife here," he turned and pointed to the elderly lady standing beside him. "And myself are here looking for our daughter." The woman was looking at her husband while he spoke. Tears slipped out of her eyes and ran down her cheeks. The woman paid no attention to her wet face. It was as if she had done this many times before.

The sheriff jumped up and motioned with his hand offering each one a chair. The couple hesitated and the woman waited for her husband to sit down first. Then she sat down.

The sheriff asked them to tell him all about their daughter.

The husband hunched over and sat with his elbows on his knees looking down at the floor. He spoke slowly in a sorrowful voice. "Our daughter is just a young girl. She met a neighbor boy and decided she would like to marry him. But he was not ready to settle down with anyone. It was a few months ago she ran away from home. Ma kept saying our daughter was gaining weight and might have been carrying a child."

The woman spoke in a desperate voice, "We've searched every where. We have spent all of the money we had. Some days we go through alleys looking into garbage cans just so we can eat."

Suddenly the sheriff was feeling sick to his stomach. His face felt flushed and his hands were sweaty. He had a thought but he had to make sure before he said anything.

He wanted to help. He suggested they go over to the boarding house and get some food. "Tell the cook I sent you."

He continued by saying, "I'll start a search right away. You'll have to tell me her name and describe her to me."

The girl's father started first.

"Her name is Ruby Morrison , she is fifteen years old. Her hair is dark brown, it hangs to her waist. She has dark brown eyes."

The woman was so full of grief and sadness. Her heart ached to see and touch her daughter. She spoke next and said, "My little girl was always a good girl, she was very quiet. She never talked a lot. The last time we saw her she was wearing a brown dress with a coat one of her brothers had out grown. We didn't have money enough to buy her a new coat."

The mother's voice was becoming almost a whisper. She was getting choked up.

"We stopped at a homestead where she had worked for her board and room. They told us she left one night during the night time hours. She was wearing a brown dress that was too big for her. But the woman of the homestead also said she looked like she was carrying a child. The girl hardly ever talked."

The mother stopped talking and covered her face with her hands.

The sheriff stood up and slowly walked around the desk. He put one hand on the desk, bent over and put the other hand on the father's shoulder.

The sheriff was completely overwhelmed by all he had just heard from a family in so much pain.

He said, "Sir, take your wife to the boarding house dining room and get yourselves a good meal." He stood up straight and continued, "I'll start looking for your daughter."

The sheriff knew exactly where he was going to go first. The couple walked out of his office. When the door closed he turned to his deputy and yelled in an angry voice, "Get my horse saddled now."

The deputy had just tied the sheriff's horse to the hitching post. Sheriff Les with his long stride opened the door so hard it slammed against the inside wall and stayed open. He put one hand on the hitching post and jumped over the end on it. His foot was in the stirrup and he was astride his horse.

He had not noticed how strong the wind was while riding in the shelter of the buildings in town. Out in the open area he realized the weather was threatening with rain coming.

## ⁓ Chapter 50 ⁓

Rose heard the door open wide and slam shut loudly. She jumped up from behind her desk in her office at the hospital. In the dark open door of her office a large figure appeared. Rose's eyes were trying to adjust to see the face of the man. The sheriff was dripping with rain water.

The sheriff spoke in a deep voice of uncertainty and compassion.

He said, "Rose, I think we have the parents," he paused and then said, "of that young girl that died in your hospital." He took in a deep breath and went on, "By the time they got to my office after traveling a long distance they had no money to buy food. I sent them to get something to eat."

The first reaction from Rose was silence. She tried to comprehend what the sheriff had just said, "Are you sure? What did they say?"

As Rose spoke her voice became louder. She stopped for a minute while staring into the sheriff's eyes. "Did you tell them about the baby dying?"

"No, Rose, I did not tell them anything. You told me about the brown dress she was wearing. Also a boy's jacket. They also told me about the brown dress and the boy's jacket she was wearing. I have a feeling the girl was their daughter. You will have to talk to them."

"Rose, you have to tell them what happened to their daughter."

The sheriff had no idea.

Rose was sure the secret was safe. She would not reveal the secret. Not for a long time. The only other person who knew the secret would never tell.

Blue Sky would die before she told a living soul.

Rose spoke softly to the sheriff saying, "Please tell the couple to come and see me as soon as they can."

The sheriff left with some knowledge the couple would learn the truth of what happened to their daughter.

## ∽ Chapter 51 ∾

Nothing could have prepared Rose to see the hurt a parent endures to find they have lost a child.

The following morning after Sheriff Les had visited Rose, the father and mother of the young girl came to see her at the hospital.

"Our daughters name was Ruby Morrison." The father said sadly.

Rose was reluctant and careful of what she said. She told them about their daughter's long and hard labor.

The couple starred at Rose while listening to her every word. They asked for two things. First, they wanted to talk to the woman who delivered their daughter's baby. Then they asked what the baby was.

"The baby was a boy." Rose whispered.

"I will contact Blue Sky. I will also take you out to the Higgens' Cemetery where your daughter and her baby are buried." Rose said quietly.

Blue Sky entered the hospital knowing the young girl's parents were waiting for her. Rose was sitting behind her desk. Blue Sky walked in the office, and stood beside her. She looked at each one and could see the anguish on their faces.

"I am so sorry for your loss. I have delivered many babies. Your daughter was only a girl. I tried very hard to save her and her baby boy. She was very small and the labor and birth very difficult. She did not speak at all while she was here" Blue Sky's voice was gentle as she tried to give some comfort to the couple.

The mother sat looking at her husband waiting for him to say something to give her some relief, but he too was mourning and could find no comfort to give her.

Rose stood up and said, "I have Ruby's brown dress and jacket if you would like it?"

"Yes, yes," the mother said with no hesitation in a raspy voice.

Blue Sky left the room and returned carrying a brown dress and a boy's jacket. The mother reached out and took it and put the dress against her chest.

The mother looked at Rose and asked, "What was my Ruby and the child buried in?"

Rose answered, "A pretty dress of mine and the baby was wrapped in a new blanket." She stopped for a minute then said slowly, "We laid the baby on her chest and wrapped her arms around him."

The sobs could be heard down the halls of the hospital.

The secret was kept.

The next few minutes was a gathering of all of the employees coming into Rose's office to give comfort to this mother and father. Arms were encircling them and pouring out love.

Before Rose could stop Mary, she came into the office after hearing the loud sounds of crying.

She was carrying a beautiful brown eyed baby boy. Blue Sky asked Mary if she could take the baby and she started to the door with him, when Blue Sky heard a voice say, "May I hold the baby? Blue Sky quickly looked at Rose. Rose raised her hand toward the baby and said. "Of course you can hold Mary's baby."

Blue Sky gently laid the baby into Ruby Morrison's mother's arms. She bent over and kissed him lovingly on his forehead. The baby opened his eyes and looked directly at the woman holding him. Then she carefully handed the baby to her husband and said, "He has eyes just like Ruby's."

Blue Sky reached for the baby and left the room immediately with him.

# ❧ *Chapter 52* ❧

Rose's voice was firm when she asked for her buggy to be brought to the hospital. She felt unsettled and guilty. She also sent word to the sheriff to come to the cemetery.

Her mind kept going back to thinking this couple could give the baby nothing but a hard life. They had no money, no education. How would they care for him?

Rose questioned the couple while riding with her to the cemetery.

"Where do you live? What occupation do you have? How many other children do you have?" She wanted to know everything about them.

The man seemed eager to answer Rose's questions. The woman sat with her hands folded and her head down.

He started telling Rose, "I have about twenty acres of land, about fifty miles from here. I farm with my two sons. Ruby was our only girl. We have no money left after the land payment."

Tears filled Rose's eyes as she looked straight ahead, afraid the couple would see them and wonder why.

Arriving at the cemetery, Sheriff Les, Henry, Toby and Blue Sky were already standing at Ruby Morrison's grave site.

The parents stood with their arms around each other. The sheriff stood next to them talking softly. He mentioned to them, Rose had ordered a stone and now that they knew their daughter's name, her name, and baby boy would be written on it.

Sheriff Les opened a small bible and began to read. Then with no warning, Ruby Morrison's mother dropped to her knees. Her father bent his knees and knelt beside his wife.

Rose Donlin was at the breaking point as she took a step toward them, and then she felt a hand on her arm. Blue Sky stopped her from taking another step. She looked straight into

*Rose's Dream Fulfilled*

Rose's eyes. It was a piercing look and Rose knew she would not tell their secret.

The good-bys were extremely hard as the Morrisons left with the sheriff to return to their home with so much sorrow.

The sheriff had several instructions from Rose when he arrived back into Oklahoma City. First he needed to stop at the bank and give John a letter she had written. A large envelope of money the sheriff was to give the couple before they started home. Also he needed to stop at the land title office and with the money John was to give him, he was to pay off the mortgage the Morrison family owed on their homestead.

The message Sheriff Les gave to the family, the gifts came from a church in Oklahoma City.

The Morrison family would never look in garbage cans for food. Rose was determined to watch over them.

## ⌒ Chapter 53 ⌒

When leaving the cemetery Henry crawled up into the buggy beside Rose. She whispered to him to take her out to the place where their cabin would be built. Her day had no happiness in it at all. But now, being with Henry made everything better. She was feeling anxious for the cabin to be ready when they were married.

"Henry, Rose said slowly and deliberately, "I am ready to start drilling for oil and I'm asking if you would be in charge?"

"Oh Rose, I would do anything for you. Of course, I will. I want to marry you now." He answered, then, added, "Please marry me today, Rose."

Higgens' Hospital

Higgens' Library